THE AMISH COWBOY'S LITTLE MATCHMAKERS

AMISH COWBOYS OF MONTANA
BOOK IX

ADINA SENFT

Cover design by Carpe Librum Book Design. Images used under license. Published by Moonshell Books, Inc., PO Box 752, Redwood Estates, CA 95044.

The Amish Cowboy's Little Matchmakers / Adina Senft—1st ed.

ISBN 978-1-963929-11-9 R020125

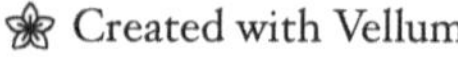 Created with Vellum

"Any book that can both entertain and leave me thinking is a book worth reading! Adina Senft is quickly becoming one of my favorite writers of Amish fiction.... Senft's characters are beautifully developed, [and] will move you to both laugh and cry."

— CHRISTIAN FICTION ADDICTION

Children bring their parents close to each other. Parents bring their children close to God. —Mountain Home Amish proverb

The Millers at the Wild Rose Amish Inn

- Rachel Zook Miller and Luke Hertzler (engaged to be married in October)
- Tobias Miller, widower, father of twins Gracie and Benny
- Gideon Miller
- Susanna Miller and Stephen Kurtz (also engaged to be married in October)
- Seth Miller

The Millers on the Circle M Ranch

- Reuben and Naomi Glick Miller
- Daniel and Lovina Wengerd Lapp Miller, Joel
- Adam Miller and Kate Weaver (engaged to be married in December)
- Zach Miller and Ruby Wengerd (engaged)
- Malena Miller and Alden Stolzfus (courting)
- Noah and Rebecca Miller King
- Joshua and Sara Fischer Miller, Nathan
- Deborah Miller (age 1)

The Keims on the Bow K Ranch

- Josiah and Kathryn Keim
- Sylvia Keim (28)
- Sharon (22) and Bethany (21) Keim, Josiah's nieces
- Stephen Kurtz, ranch foreman
- Mark Steiner (26), Pete and Danny Troyer, ranch hands

THE AMISH COWBOY'S LITTLE MATCHMAKERS

MOUNTAIN HOME, MONTANA

The Wild Rose Amish Inn
Monday, June 13

"YOUR DAADI USED to say that a barn raising was ninety percent muscle and ten percent miracle." Dat adjusted his tool belt around his waist, which made Benny Miller wish with all his seven-year-old heart that he could wear a tool belt, too.

"Is it, Dat?" his twin sister Grace asked as she trotted beside them across the freshly cut grass that was supposed to be lawn, but was mostly meadow full of hay and Queen Anne's Lace and yarrow and dozens of kinds of bugs and butterflies.

"Do you remember when we built the barn on the Four Winds Ranch in New Mexico?" When Benny shook his head, Dat nodded. "I suppose not—you two were just toddlers—and it was just before—" His throat seemed to close up, but Benny knew what he meant.

Before Mamm had left them and gone to *Gott in Himmel.*

Dat gripped Benny's shoulder wordlessly as the sun gleamed out through the midsummer notch in the mountains that surrounded the Siksika Valley. "Here they come. Open the gate."

Benny and Gracie ran to obey, feeling all the honor of being the ones to unlatch the new gate Alden Stolzfus had made, to welcome their neighbors in. Instead of taking you into the parking lot of the Wild Rose Amish Inn, the new lane took a visitor out past Mamm's garden and down the gentle slope to the building site. A barn had stood there once, back in the olden days, but Dat and Luke Hertzler, Mammi's intended, had let Benny help them tear it all out. Noah King and his crew had poured the foundation as soon as the ground had dried up from the blizzard ... and now it was time to build.

It took the strength of both he and Gracie to walk the big bar gate open and latch it on the other side. And the *Gmay* rolled through, led by crew foreman Noah King and his wife Rebecca, the buggies bearing Amish families from both districts, all come to help the Millers build their barn. While the twins stood watch at the gate, Onkel Gideon and Onkel Seth acted as hostlers, lining up the buggies and unhitching the horses to turn them loose in the pasture.

"Onkel Reuben!" Benny called, waving as their relatives from the Circle M Ranch passed in a caravan of buggies and wagons filled with equipment and supplies and food. "Gracie, look, they brought our buggy!"

"And the horses! Adam's driving Murphy. Mamm says he and Kate are going to get married in December."

Benny just snorted like one of the horses. Trust a girl to drag in a wedding instead of joining in the excitement of a barn raising!

Here came the bishop with his wife Sadie and daughter Ruby, who was courting with Benny's cousin Zachary. And here were Josiah and Kathryn Keim, with their daughter Sylvia and her two cousins Bethany and Sharon, followed by their ranch hands—Aendi Susanna's boyfriend Stephen Kurtz, Mark Steiner, and Pete and Danny from Colorado, who followed on cutting horses, their saddlebags bulging with hammers and tools.

He and Gracie exchanged a grin. Of course they knew Sylvia would come to help the women with the *Middaag* meal, but there had been a little niggling possibility that she might be sick and throw all their plans out the window.

But now their plans were safe. They just had to wait for the right moment to put them into action.

After the first big wave of helpers had come through, the twins ran down to join Dat. As the eldest man of the family, it was his place to say a prayer before work began. Even Benny knew that if you didn't ask the Lord to bless an undertaking, you were taking a risk—and with something as important as a barn, no one was willing to do that.

"Lieber Gott in Himmel," Dat began, his voice carrying over the men, the piles of lumber on the ground, and the big stack of trusses at one end, "we thank You for the *gut* weather You've sent us today, with not a snowflake in sight."

Some of the *Youngie* chuckled, though the blizzard two weeks ago had been no joke.

"We thank You for the willingness in the heart of every man and woman, boy and girl who came to lend their hands and skills in this undertaking. We pray that You would bless our efforts so that the work of our hands would glorify Your name, and protect and keep every animal and person who finds shelter in this building. We ask all this in the name of our elder Brother, Jesus Christ."

Benny could almost hear the indrawn breaths of a hundred or so men as the crowd flowed into motion. Noah, as foreman, divided them into crews, each led by an experienced carpenter to manage and instruct his men. Benny ran to join the crew led by Onkel Seth, who as the youngest man on the property, was responsible for the helpers under fourteen.

"All right, boys," he said, gathering them round. "Your job is to keep this site clean."

Some of the older ones groaned. To them, keeping things clean probably meant washing and scrubbing.

"Looks like you've never done this before," Seth said with a grin. Then he sobered. "This job matters. All we need is for the bishop to step on a sixteen-penny nail and have it go straight through his boot sole and into his foot. Because then look out."

Benny didn't even want to think about that. His cousins Adam, Zach, and Joshua's wife Sara were all experienced EMTs —they'd brought their emergency packs today, just in case— but he wondered if even they were up to the job of pulling a nail out of Little Joe Wengerd's foot when he was howling like a bear.

"Our job is to pick up every nail that falls, inspect it, and if it's *gut*, send it back up to be used. If it's bent or damaged, it goes in that galvanized bucket." He pointed. "The next thing is wood scraps. We'll be setting the studs sixteen inches on center. Anything sixteen inches or more goes back in the working pile to be used as blocks. Anything less goes in the kindling pile for the Inn's woodstove."

"How much is sixteen inches?" Benny asked.

"Good question. Short answer—on most of you, from the ground to your knee. Long answer—to be certain, borrow my tape measure and see exactly where that falls on you. Pick up everything and put it in its pile. The littlest boys can practice using a hammer on the scrap blocks and ends if they want. But you bigger ones, I want you on patrol all day long, keeping this work site safe. *Verschteh?*"

"*Verschtanne!*" Benny hollered.

Gracie ran up, out of breath. "What's do we understand? What can I do?"

"You're a girl," one of the older boys said scornfully. "Go back to the kitchen."

"The kitchen's in the house, and I live here," she informed him, her cheeks reddening. "I want to help."

"Girls don't help with building," the boy said. "That's a man's job."

"There's only one man here, and that's *mei onkel*," she snapped. "You're just a *boy*." She appealed to Seth. "I can help, can't I?"

"Where does Mammi want you?" he asked soberly, clearly ignoring her tone in view of the greater good. "Much as we can use every pair of hands, I'm thinking she does, too. Because there's a bunch of *Maedscher* who have never been here, and it looks like they might need some guidance."

"But I want to help with building."

"I know, and I'm glad of it," Seth said. "But see how Noah assigned leaders to every crew? Guess which one doesn't have a leader."

He gestured with his chin to where the group of little girls were milling around where the tables were being set up for lunch, getting underfoot. A game of tag had even broken out.

"They need to get the tablecloths on," Gracie said in disapproving surprise, sounding every bit like Miss Hannah, their former schoolteacher at the little *Schulhaus* by the Circle M.

"Go show them what to do, Gracie," Seth said.

She marched off, and Benny marveled at how close she'd

come to a meltdown before Seth headed it off at the pass. He was *good.*

If he thought he'd worked hard during the move from the Four Winds, or even during the renovations to the Inn, Benny realized he had only been practicing for this. By midmorning, when the *kaffee* came out in big silver urns and a dozen plates of cowboy cake, bread and peanut butter spread, and sliced fruit had been laid on the tables (complete with tablecloths) on the big flat meadow between Mammi's garden and the Inn, the four sides of the first floor were already up. Benny got so he could spot a nail at ten feet, and as for scraps, well, he'd soon found out why Dat had wanted him to wear the work gloves he'd been given for *Grischtdaag.*

Gracie found him with his mouth full of cowboy cake, attempting to drink a glass of milk at the same time.

"We have to start the plan," she whispered, for there were any number of people crowded all around the tables.

"Mmph," he agreed, and swallowed mightily. Despite best efforts, they hadn't settled on an actual plan, just discarded about a dozen bad ones. "Can you see them?"

"Onkel Tobias is getting a cup of coffee from that bossy-pants Susan Bontrager. That's a shame. Sylvia is pouring coffee all the way at the other end."

Bad luck. "Maybe when she takes the urn back to the house, we could get him to help her."

She gave him a pitying look. "She'd just laugh at him and tell him to get back to work. No, I think we'd better wait for lunch. If they both have full stomachs, it might be easier to get them to do what we want."

"They need to do something together, but she can't climb up in the rafters and he can't do dishes. He's got a crew to manage."

"I'll think of something. You think, too. We still have time."

He nodded, and swiped a couple of oatmeal chocolate chip cookies to sustain him until lunch. One crew at a time took a break, while the other three kept on laying the floor joists, the subfloor, and at last, the top layer. Noah had explained it all last night at supper, when he and Rebecca and his brother Simon and his fiancée Susan had come over to review the last-minute details.

By lunchtime, the floor was complete, and two crews had finished putting in bats of insulation between the ground floor studs, and started work on the shear walls. Benny and his uncle's crew were kept hopping then, because not only did nails fall outside, now they had to be alert to the ones being dropped inside, on the big concrete pad. At least it was easier to see them there, and they made a *ping!* you could hear.

And then came a *clang!* and an exclamation from above that got the attention of all his crew. "That was a hammer!" Benny said.

"I'll get it!"

"*Neh*, I'll get it!"

Benny, who happened to be nearest, snatched up the hammer an inch ahead of a big blond thirteen-year-old, and ran for the twelve-foot ladder leaning in the big square hole where the staircase up to the bunkhouse would go. He squinted against the sun on the upper floor to find the tool's owner.

"Hey!" Josiah Keim called. "That's mine. Send it up with—"

But Benny was already on the way up. It would only be a few steps along the line of studs to reach Josiah. This ladder was the tallest he'd ever been on, but he stuck the hammer through the front fall of his pants and used both hands to climb, the way Dat had taught him.

"Benny, wait for me there. That hammer's not secure."

Was that Dat? The sun was in his eyes and he blinked. Just a few more rungs and he'd be out of the glare.

"Benny, look out!"

He froze, thinking something was falling on him. And then he heard the awful thump of a hammer hitting flesh, then a second clang as it landed on the concrete directly below. With a gasp, he felt all around his waistband as far as he could reach with one hand.

It was gone.

Below, the big blond boy lay face down on the concrete, the hammer that had fallen out of Benny's pants lying two feet from his head.

❧   2   ❧

TOBIAS MILLER HAD THOUGHT his heart might stop at the sight of his seven-year-old son climbing that ladder. But it stopped for sure and certain when the hammer fell out of Benny's pants.

By that time, he'd jumped up from the wall he'd been putting together on the upper floor, and both he and Josiah arrived at the top of the ladder at the same time. Gripping a rung of the ladder, his boy looked up, his eyes already filling with tears.

"I didn't mean to drop it, Dat." His voice wobbled.

"I know you didn't, *mei Sohn*," he said, surprised his own wasn't wobbling, too. "You head back down, now, and run and find one of your cousins. We need an EMT."

Benny went down the ladder so fast that Tobias had to take a deep breath so that he didn't holler and distract him into a fall of his own. He and Josiah descended, then gently pushed the crowd of boys out of the way enough to kneel by the fallen one, who was trying to get his knees under him. Josiah slid the offending hammer into its loop on his tool belt, looking grim as Paul Petersheim, the boy's father, jogged up.

"What happened?"

Josiah told him, with his usual economy of words. The final sentence was barely out of his mouth when Adam Miller jogged up, his red backpack with the white cross slung over one shoulder, Benny at his heels.

"What have we got? Benny says a hammer hit him?"

"Josiah says it was his hammer," Paul told him. "Hit a knot and lost his grip."

"My boy picked it up and was climbing the ladder to bring it back to him, and it fell and hit Terence standing below." There. Tobias could be brief, too.

Adam was already examining Terence with the gentleness of a mother, encouraging him to lie down again and sliding a pad under his head. The boy's eyes widened at the crowd of faces leaning over him. "Dat? What hit me?"

Adam shone a penlight in his eyes. "Where does it hurt, Terence?"

"Something hit me on the head."

Adam glanced at Josiah as he put the penlight away, then began an examination, his fingers gentle on the boy's skull. "Any blood on that hammer?"

Josiah examined it minutely from the claw to the end of the handle. *"Neh."*

Terence flinched under the searching fingers, and Adam parted his hair just over his ear. "Looks like your thick hair and your hat saved you from worse. But you'll have a goose egg to be proud of," he told him. "I don't feel a depression of any kind. I don't think your skull is cracked, but we don't take chances with head injuries, especially ones that knock you out even for a second. I called the firehouse.

We'll take you over to the neuro center for an X-ray, all right?"

The boy's eyes filled with fear as he looked over at his father. "Dat?"

"It's all right, Terence. Adam will look after you. Mamm and I will follow in the buggy."

"But your crew."

"It was my hammer did the wrong," Josiah said, patting his shoulder. "I'll do your dat's work as well as my own."

The EMT van arrived and the child was loaded on a gurney. When the van pulled away, one of Paul's other sons ran to catch the Petersheim horse and hitch it up.

As Josiah encouraged the others to get back to work, Tobias took Benny aside. "Tell me what happened."

Benny gulped and then took a big breath and told him. "One of the other boys said it was the handle that whacked him, not the metal part."

"We can be thankful for that. I'll speak with Paul tonight to find out how the boy is. And then tomorrow at first light, you'll go and apologize."

"But it was an accident, Dat!"

"It was, but Terence was still hurt and you are still sorry. Aren't you?"

Benny flushed and looked down. *"Ja."*

"If you don't go, what will Terence think?"

Now his son met his eyes. "I don't know. I never saw him except at church."

"But on your first meeting outside of that, look what happened. You and he are both part of the *Gmay, mei Sohn.* Remember what Paul told the Colossians?"

Benny shook his head.

"He was talking about the parts of the body. *That there*

should be no schism in the body; but that the members should have the same care one for another."

"What's a schism?"

"Like a ditch in the pasture you have to jump over. And so that we don't keep falling in that schism, we have to let Terence know that we care about him."

Something in Benny's expression told Tobias he had just learned something, even if he didn't like it very much. Best to let him sit with it and say no more.

All the same, at *Middagessen* it was difficult for Tobias to field all the questions about what had happened while trying to keep an eye on Benny. It was a toss-up whether his boy would hide and avoid people, or try to bluff it out and make a pest of himself. Tobias barely knew what he was eating. Somehow he ate a full plate, though he couldn't have told anyone what was on it.

One of the *Maedschere* removed his plate and invited him to the dessert buffet. But Tobias drew the line. He needed to set the example and get back to the barn. He was just draining his glass of lemonade when he saw Gracie walking slowly down the gentle slope from the Inn toward the dessert table, carrying a three-layer chocolate cake bigger than her head. Beside her walked Sylvia Keim with a huge clear plastic bowl full of what looked like banana pudding.

Some instinct propelled Tobias out of his seat.

"Gracie, wait—let me—stop, *liebling*."

His little girl looked up at the sound of his voice. Stopped obediently, though she was clearly confused. The plate dipped —the cake—

"Gracie!"

He vaulted over two children sitting on the grass with their plates, both hands outstretched to field the cake. At that moment, Sylvia's shoe slipped into a gopher hole and she lost her grip on the bowl. She fell into Gracie—Gracie went down —both cake and banana pudding cartwheeled into the air and came down on top of them. A wave of pudding slopped out onto the grass just as Tobias barreled across it. Both his feet slid out from under him and he landed on top of Sylvia—or rather, on top of the half of the cake that had landed on Sylvia.

A dozen children whooped in horrified delight at the spectacle.

Dazed, he managed to slide off the body under him and into the pool of pudding on the grass. Gracie, covered in chocolate, burst into tears, howling in the ear-splitting way she had when she was truly in pain.

"Gracie, *Liewi*, where does it hurt?" He crawled over to her. Two children in the space of an hour. He couldn't bear it. "Gracie?"

"Sylvia's caaaaake!" she roared, tears and snot and frosting all running together down her scarlet face. Nothing remained of the cake except the plate clutched in both chocolate-covered hands. "It's ruuuuuuined!"

She hadn't been cut by a shard of broken porcelain. He inhaled in relief and sucked in a glob of banana pudding that chose that moment to drop out of his hair.

The little boys were already making off with chunks of cake. One enterprising *Kind* dipped his in the pudding on the grass before hightailing it away.

He removed the plate from her grip and gathered her into his arms. "It's all right, *Liebling*. It's just a cake. You're not hurt, are you?"

"It's not just a cake," she blubbered. "It's Sylvia's special double fudge cake and I *ruined* it!"

Sylvia pushed herself up so that she leaned on one hand in

the pudding puddle, and thoughtfully scooped a chunk of cake off her skirt. She took a big bite. "Mm. This is really *gut,* if I say so myself. Try it, Gracie."

Which sent his daughter into another paroxysm of tears.

"No, I mean it," Sylvia persisted.

Good grief, couldn't the woman see how distressed and upset his child was?

She popped a bit of cake with a nice dollop of frosting into Gracie's open mouth. His daughter's eyes unsqueezed and she gawked at the woman.

"See? No matter what shape it's in, it's still *gut.* Here, Tobias. Have some." And she offered him a chunk as big as her palm, also liberally frosted.

He glared at her in outrage, but he might as well have been glaring at a mule. Unlike a mule, she widened her eyes like the *Youngie* did to indicate a person was being hopelessly slow on the uptake. His hand moved of its own volition and he accepted the cake.

Took a bite.

"Mm," he said in surprise. Double fudge cake? It would win first prize at the county fair. He eyeballed a big piece in Gracie's lap. "Are you going to eat that?"

She snatched it up and held it out of his reach. *"Ja."*

And then there was a free-for-all as a waiting horde of *Kinner* swooped in to get theirs. So much for portion control— it was all Sylvia could do to keep the bits that actually had dirt and grass on them out of their hands and toss them into the near-empty plastic bowl.

"Kumm mit, you three." Mamm couldn't keep a straight face to save her life as she helped Sylvia to her feet. "Susanna, take that bowl and rinse it," she said to his sister, who was practically weeping with laughter. "Sylvia,

Gracie, Tobias, come up to the *Haus*. I'm going to hose you all off. Chocolate is impossible to get out—I'm afraid your clothes will have to be relegated to barn work after this."

"At least now we have a barn." Gracie was recovering. She took Tobias's chocolatey hand in one of hers and Sylvia's in the other. "Come on."

His funny little *Dochder*. Weeping as though her heart would break one minute, and cheerful as a cricket the next.

As they climbed the slope toward the hose bib at the far end of the family section of the Inn, here came Benny at a dead run. "At least you didn't hurt anybody with that cake," he told his sister. "Mammi, can I hose Dat off?"

"*Neh*, you may not," Tobias said hastily. He wouldn't put it past him to soak him head to foot, and Sylvia too.

"I will do the hosing," Mamm said, and stood by her word. Once she had the worst of it sluiced off, she took Sylvia inside to dry herself and borrow a dress.

Gracie kept him company on the deck in the sun, the two of them dribbling water on the warm planks until it was safe to go in and change. "Are you mad at me, Dat?" she asked in a small voice. "I didn't mean to ruin Sylvia's cake."

"Of course I'm not mad." He put an arm around her, and when Benny claimed his other side, somehow mysteriously wet to the knees, he slid his other arm around him. "And Sylvia didn't look very mad, either. I'm glad she got to eat some of her cake, anyway."

"Are you mad at me?" Benny wanted to know.

"Of course not." He gave his sturdy little shoulders a squeeze. "Gracie, Benny and I are going to see Terence Petersheim tomorrow. First thing, before the work gets started here. Would you like to come with us?"

"Now that we have a buggy and our horses, we can all go." She sounded as though this had just occurred to her.

"Maybe Sylvia can come with us," Benny said.

Tobias blinked in surprise. "Sylvia? She didn't drop anything on the poor boy."

"*Neh*, but it was her father's hammer. And her cake."

He did his best to keep a straight face. "I think Sylvia has had enough of hammers, cakes, and Millers for one day," he told them.

"Oh, I don't know about that." Looking fresh and neat in one of Susanna's dresses, Sylvia came out the back door and smiled over her shoulder at them. The sun touched her face and a dimple deep enough to press a fingertip into appeared and disappeared in her cheek. "One is necessary, one is a treat, and one keeps life interesting. I wish I knew which was which."

Laughing, she strolled away, and Mamm stuck her head out of the door. "Gracie, Tobias, come on. The day is only half over and you can't go back to work soaking wet. Benny, go tell Noah that Dat will be down in ten minutes."

Benny ran off, catching up with Sylvia and walking with her the rest of the way.

"Tobias?"

He jerked his gaze away from the pair and followed his mother and daughter into the house.

3

SYLVIA KEIM HAD SEEN MORE than one barn raising, but aside from the cake catastrophe, there was something about this one that seemed extra special.

Maybe it was the fact that the Millers had been without a barn since they'd moved in at the tail end of winter. For an Amish family, that was a hardship, since there had been nowhere to keep their horses, and consequently no buggy for transportation. They'd had to leave both at the Circle M. More important, they had nowhere to hold church. Little Joe had informed the district earlier in the year that since the Wild Rose Amish Inn was essentially a business, he would wait until they built the barn before he added the family into the church rotation.

She had to admire the efficiency of Noah King's management of the whole process. For someone younger than she, he had carpentry skills you just didn't see every day. Even with the setback of the blizzard a couple of weeks ago, supplies had arrived and been staged in the order they'd be needed. The concrete had been poured and given time to cure. And now the building was so far along that two crews swarmed over the roof, spacing out the trusses while two more worked behind them, one with insulation and one with sheathing.

She could hardly wait for a tour once everything was complete and the last finishing nail had been driven into the trim inside. Mind you, there would be no reason for anyone to give her a tour. With a sigh, she went into the Inn's kitchen to wash the dishes from the afternoon *Kaffee* break.

"You don't have to do that, Sylvia," Rachel Miller said, coming in with a tub of coffee cups. "Susanna and I can do it."

"You've had enough to do," Sylvia told her with a smile. "You've earned your own cup of coffee, and I think there is still a plastic container full of cookies left. Peanut butter chocolate chip."

Rachel groaned. "I'll have to join Benny's cleanup crew. All that bending and stretching to pick up nails and scrap will wear it off. Where is Susanna, anyway?"

"Now that the men are in the final stretch, I think she took some of the *Kinner* down to the creek to keep them busy until their parents are ready to go home."

"Ah. Well, I'll take your advice." Rachel spoke over her shoulder. "Naomi, *kumm mit* out on the patio with the others. It's time for a break for ourselves."

The two sisters-in-law deposited their tubs of dirty dishes, collected coffee and cookies and went out the kitchen door to the sunny patio. Sylvia could see them through the window over the sink, settling in the sun for a few minutes of quiet with some of the other women with whom they were close—Sadie the bishop's wife, Rose Stoltzfus from the quilt shop, and Kate King, Noah's mother.

None of them except Rachel and Naomi had grown up together. Their buddy bunches were scattered far and wide.

And yet these women seemed to fit together as though their four separate paths had brought them here for the purpose of friendship—the kind Sylvia was coming to see that women depended on as they grew older and their families made homes of their own. Rachel had even found love in the last place she'd expected—full circle, back in the Siksika Valley where she'd grown up. Sylvia didn't know Rose's story well, only that she'd been widowed and that it hadn't been a happy marriage. She had three wonderful *Kinner*, though, and her son Alden was courting Malena Miller. Sylvia was pretty sure an engagement wouldn't be too long in coming.

She didn't envy Malena, exactly, or even Rachel. Envy was a sin. But oh ... how wonderful it would be to spend the day at a work frolic and then climb into a buggy and go home beside a man who loved you.

"What was that big sigh for?" Her mother, Kathryn Keim, lugged a plastic tub full of plates across to the counter, staging them behind the cups Sylvia was washing as fast as she could.

"Oh, nothing." Not for worlds would she let the truth escape her lips.

Mamm glanced out the window. "I suppose they deserve a rest. I could use one, too. Your cousins are on their way up with the last of the dishes. Then we can box them up and put them back in the bench wagon."

It stood in the parking lot, well out of the way of the spaces provided for the *Englisch* guests' vehicles. Most of them seemed to be gone, the guests probably fishing and hiking and holidaying. Susanna had said that they even had a pair of painters staying for a week.

"Do the *Youngie* have plans after the work is done?" Mamm picked up a towel and got started on the draining cups.

"I don't know," Sylvia admitted, applying herself with fresh energy to the plates. "Not likely word would get to me anyway. I'm not involved so much anymore in their doings."

"You know how I feel about that, *Dochder*. If you kept company with the *Youngie* more, you'd stay young."

"Twenty-eight isn't old, Mamm." Though watching eighteen-year-olds experiencing courtship for the first time certainly made her feel that way sometimes.

She'd had a few dates, it was true, and had even been courted once, but the young man had ended up marrying someone else and moving away. She'd been happy for him, and relieved it hadn't been her having to move. She loved the valley and wanted to live here always.

"But I know you'd rather be out there on the patio or in here doing dishes than doing whatever the young girls are up to."

She'd rather be talking to Rachel Miller and picking up wisps of news and crumbs of facts about Tobias, gleaning kernels like Ruth in the field, to grind up later and give herself something to sustain her when she hungered fruitlessly for a future that might include him.

"I don't know if that's true," she said mildly. "I think I've already made enough of a spectacle of myself today."

Mamm chuckled and began to stack the cups in their sturdy box. "Much as I was glad you didn't hurt yourself, I have to say it was the craziest thing I've seen since the day those twins let the goats out just before church."

Sylvia groaned at the memory. "I never saw the Zook brothers move so fast in all my life."

"Well, neither one is exactly old, you know. Willard is the elder, but Zeke is younger than I am."

This did not seem like a very good argument. "He's fifty, Mamm."

"The prime of life."

"For some, maybe. Do not go getting ideas that involve me."

"Willard admires you, I know that."

Sylvia lost her grip on her self-control and snorted. "Willard Zook admires a fine breeding nanny-goat, or a good milk-producing cow, or a hen that lays double yolks. That's not much of a recommendation." She glared at her mother. "And don't say one word about breeding."

Mamm bit back what Sylvia was certain she had been about to say. "You'd make such a *gut* mother," she said instead. "You have that knack with the *Kinner*. It's real sweet to see."

"If I do, then I'll wait for a future father to appear in *Gottes gut* time. Because I know for a fact he's neither of the Zook brothers."

"You could do worse. Their place is paid for, and their artisan cheeses get orders from all over the west, I hear."

"Mamm. They're confirmed bachelors. Everyone knows that if one of them did get married, his wife might as well have two husbands. Twice as much laundry, and twice as many dishes. Twice as many disagreements, too, probably."

"All right, all right." Mamm hefted the box of cups onto one hip and went out to the wagon in a virtuous silence. As if her presence had left a vacuum, Bethany and Sharon, Sylvia's two cousins who were helping out at their ranch for the summer, breezed in.

"Here you are, working away by yourself." Bethany opened drawers until she found the dishtowels, and handed one to her sister. They got busy on the plates while Mamm came in with two more empty boxes.

"Not any longer," Sylvia said cheerfully. Her cousins always seemed to fill a room with chatter and laughter. "How does the roof look?"

"Nearly done," Bethany said with a glance at her sister. "What did Mark call it?"

"Dried in," Sharon said. "Onkel Josiah said the crew from the ranch could come back tomorrow and help finish the roof. They've got the siding done on both ends, too."

"Once the walls are up and the roof is on," Mamm said, the plates clanking into their places as she packed them, "and the weather can't get in, the barn will be as good as done. Doors and windows aren't so difficult to install if it's just the Miller brothers doing it."

Here was a tiny grain Sylvia could glean. She savored the picture it made.

"Mark says it's not the structure that takes so long, it's the finish work," Sharon said.

"Mark says ... Mark says," Bethany mocked. "You're like a parrot. Do you remember every single word Mark says?"

"Only the important ones." Sharon glanced at her aunt from under her lashes. "I like to learn. And learning what goes into building a house or a barn could be important someday."

Bethany just laughed. "It's not like you'd be on a crew."

"Just watching them work," Mamm teased her. "Besides, Mark is too old for you."

"He is not!" Sharon wiped fiercely at a defenseless plate. "I'm twenty-two. Four years is nothing."

"I agree with Aendi Kathryn," Bethany said primly. "Calvin Yoder, now. He's much closer to you in age."

With a squeal, Sharon snapped her sister with the dishtowel, making the younger girl jump and howl. Laughing, the two girls hefted a box each and took the clean dishes out to the wagon.

"Those girls," Mamm said, shaking her head and smiling. "I can't keep up with them."

"They are boy crazy, for sure and certain."

"But they did have one thing right. Mark is smart and knowledgeable about ranching. Building too, looks like. Your father likes him. If Stephen Kurtz moves on to another job, it's likely Dat will promote him to foreman."

Sylvia wasn't sure what kind of response her mother was looking for, so she only smiled. "Maybe Sharon is on the right track, then. Do you think he likes her?"

Mamm gave her a sideways glance. "I wasn't thinking of the girls. I was thinking of you."

Sylvia's busy hands halted on the cutlery. "Me? Willard is too old, so now you're throwing me at a younger man?"

"Not that much younger. Two years is nothing. Come on, Sylvia. You can't find a single thing to complain about in Mark Steiner. He's good-looking, hardworking, and in your father's mind at least, he has a future on the ranch."

"But he's not—" Sylvia stopped herself just in time.

"Not what? As well off as Willard?"

That was as good a reason as any to throw her mother off the track. "You know money isn't everything, Mamm." She had to change the subject, quick. "Look at those *Englischers* on the Rocking Diamond. All the money in the world and they're still not satisfied. They tried to buy Sara Miller's hay farm right out from under her, remember."

"I'm glad she and Joshua were smart and didn't let them. Those Madison boys, I tell you…"

And then her mother was off and running on the subject of *Englisch* boys with big trucks and what a hazard they were to every buggy on the road, and Sylvia's secret was safe.

By the time the sun slid behind the western peaks, turning

the snow gleaming gold and lemon, the siding on the barn was nearly completed and the roof mostly dried in. The crews put away their tools while Noah made a punch list of what they'd be able to do tomorrow with the reduced number of helpers. Summer was a fine time to build a barn and get it weathertight before it snowed in September, but it was also a short season in Montana and every ranch had more work than men to do it.

Tonight, so that her father and the hands were freed up to leave for the sunset check of the late calves in the home fields, Sylvia went out to the meadow and caught the big horse that pulled the bench wagon. It was to go over to the Eicher place, where church would be the week after next.

As she led the gelding through the pasture gate, Mark Steiner led his already saddled cutting horse through, too, and closed it behind her.

"Denki," she said over her shoulder with a smile.

"Headed over to Eichers'?"

"Neh, just halfway. One of the Eicher boys will meet me at the crossroads and I'll walk back. The girls are going to help Mamm with supper. If I'm lucky, I'll arrive just as it goes on the table."

"Want a hand hitching him up?"

She eyed him curiously as she backed the big horse between the rails. "Shouldn't you be heading out? You and Stephen and the boys have four paddocks to check before dark."

"I'm going. But not until we get this guy hitched up."

We? But Sylvia wasn't about to send help away when it was offered. With each on a side, they had him hitched up in a few minutes while Mark's own horse nibbled grass. Lastly, Sylvia checked that the wagon was securely closed up and fastened, and Mark fed the reins through their channels on the driver's side.

She climbed in without waiting for assistance. "*Denki* for your help, Mark. See you at dinner."

"Sylvia, wait." He put a hand on the open door. "I wanted to ask if you were going to the volleyball game at Rose Stolzfus's on Friday night."

Thank goodness Mamm was nowhere within earshot to learn she was a prophet. "I hadn't planned to," she said slowly. "I don't get out with the *Youngie* so much anymore. Too much to do on the ranch."

"It's for all ages," he said quickly. "Not just the *Youngie*. It's Alden's birthday and he says the young marrieds and *Kinner* are welcome. Pot luck."

Maybe Tobias would be there, and bring the twins. It was only a short walk from the Inn across the bridge to Rose Stolzfus's little house in the old part of Mountain Home.

"Maybe I might," she conceded.

"If you do, it would make sense for us to ride home together."

The picture in her head of Tobias bumping the volleyball high enough for her to spike it and win a point shattered abruptly.

"Well ... yes, but ... surely there is someone you might ask instead? Sharon and Bethany need a ride, too."

He ducked his head and she could swear he blushed. "I'm asking you. It would be nice to have a little time together, is all."

"We don't have enough time together at home?"

"You know as well as I do that it's not the same thing. A dozen people all gabbing at the supper table or feeding animals isn't the same as a girl going home from some doings with a man."

A girl? She was two years older than he was. But ... hang on just a minute. Maybe she should. If Tobias were there, and he saw her get into the buggy with Mark, it might jolt him into some kind of realization.

Or maybe she was an old maid dreaming of the impossible. Other than today, when poor Gracie's cake catastrophe had made him actually see her, Tobias treated her like any member of the *Gmay*. Or like a piece of furniture that was useful in its place, but not decorative enough to get his attention.

"Sylvia? Do you need some time to think about it?"

Mark's voice brought her back to the present with a bump. "*Neh*. I think it would be very sensible to ride home together. *Denki* for asking me."

A grin spread across his face. "Great. *Denki* for saying yes. I mean—"

She gathered up the reins and smiled at him. "I know what you meant. See you at home."

By the time she reached the little bridge that spanned the creek, and turned the horse northward along Creekside Lane, she was already regretting her rash impulse.

But it was too late to take back now.

※ 4 ※

EARLY THE NEXT MORNING, Tobias expected that the number of helpers arriving would equal the number of guests at the Inn, which was about a dozen. He was thankful that most of their guests this week were fishermen, who tended to want breakfast at the same predawn hour as Amish families. It made less work for Mamm and Susanna.

"I'm actually glad the lady painters get up a little later," Mamm confided to him as she set out the corned beef hash in its baking dish, bacon and onion pie, and for those that preferred it, a buffet of oatmeal with six different kinds of nuts and fruit for toppings, as well as honey and brown sugar. "I'm also glad the crew eats at home before they all get here. Otherwise you and your brothers would be eating outside on the verandah. The table we thought looked so big in the guest dining room looks awfully small when we're fully booked."

"It could be worse," Tobias said with a smile. "Though a

picnic at five in the morning is a little unusual. I should get the twins up."

"They're up, and somewhere around," his mother said distractedly. "I've got to get the coffee—they're all waiting for it. Can you hold the door?"

He did so while she brought in the urn, then went in search of his children. Finding them nowhere in the family part of the house, and hoping they wouldn't disobey and head upstairs to intrude into the guest rooms, he went out on the verandah and called their names.

"Down here!" Noah King pulled up in his spring wagon and waved. "Looks like they're inspecting our work."

Tobias felt a chill in his stomach. "Send them up, would you? Breakfast is on the table."

He was tempted to go in search of some of that coffee himself, but something propelled him down the steps and across the grass instead. And sure enough, through the bare studs at one end of the upper floor, he spotted two little figures running for the ladder at the far end where the disaster had occurred yesterday.

With a groan, he broke into a ground-covering jog. By the time the twins had climbed down the ladder, he was standing at the bottom with his arms crossed over his chest, breathing hard, both from the run and from frustration.

"Dat!" Benny said. "We found—"

"What did I tell the two of you last night?" he asked quietly.

"Not to go up there, but—"

"Then why did you do it?"

"Because a chicken—" Gracie began.

"When I tell you not to do a thing, or not to go somewhere, I have a reason, Benjamin. Grace, be quiet. I'm speaking."

"But Dat—a chicken—"

"You both disobeyed me, and in front of our crew, too. You know what I have to do."

Gracie began to cry. "But Dat, a chicken got up there and we had to get her down!"

"No, you didn't. Chickens can fly. The point is, you disobeyed, and now you have to take the consequences."

Benny glared at him, and for a brief moment, Tobias saw his own father in his mind's eye, standing over him and listening to the perfectly rational reason for the disobedience, but punishing the disobedience all the same.

His children knew the consequences, and they got them, then and there, while poor Noah made a point of unloading his tools outside, not inside. Afterward, Gracie ran up the slope weeping. Benny refused to cry, and took off at a run into the belt of pine forest that divided the Inn's property from that of Yoder's Variety Store.

With a sigh, Tobias put his hands on his hips and looked toward the heavens. Or rather, toward the square hole where the ladder leaned, decorated by a speckled hen roosting on the topmost rung and observing him with her head tilted, as though she couldn't quite identify his species.

"I hope you're happy," he told her. "Get down from there."

But the hen, of course, did not. Well, he couldn't leave it for the crew to deal with, not to mention her little round deposits on the subfloor. She didn't object when he climbed up and collected her ... and the egg he found lying on the plywood right behind her.

"Where did you come from?" he asked her, juggling bird

and egg under one arm and negotiating the ladder with the other.

"*Denki*, but I already had breakfast," Noah said when he reached the bottom, eyeing the egg in his hand. "I didn't think your *Kinner* meant it about a chicken."

"They may be disobedient, but they do tell the truth," he said on a sigh, letting the hen go and shooing it out of the raw rectangle that would be the door to the bunkhouse stairs by the end of the week. "This place seems to be a magnet for runaway chickens."

"The *Kinner* have *gut* hearts," Noah said.

"I know. Which doesn't make punishing them easy, but it has to be done."

"Are you going after Benny?"

Tobias shook his head. "He needs some time to cool off before he can think about forgiving me." He sighed. "And I haven't even had a cup of *Kaffee* yet. Can I bring you some?"

Noah shook his head. "I have a flask full. You go on. The others should be here any minute, and a man needs some food in his belly."

After a breakfast that the fisherman raved about, but which Tobias couldn't remember five minutes after he left the table, Benny still hadn't appeared. At the barn, Tobias had a look around for him, then grimly climbed the ladder. If he'd been defiant and come up here again ...

But he hadn't. There was no one there but Simeon and Noah up in the trusses, hammering and exchanging news of Sim's wedding plans, and a second small crew with hand staplers securing the last of the insulation between the floor joists before they laid the rest of the subfloor.

When the crew broke for midmorning coffee, Tobias had had

enough. Benny had compounded his sins when Gracie had to take over his task of picking up nails and scrap, now that all the *Kinner* from yesterday were resuming their normal work at home.

As Noah and the men enjoyed cowboy cake on the veranda in the sun, he accepted a cup of coffee from his sister. "Benny hasn't been up here to the house, has he?"

Susanna shook her head. "After the lady painters left, we were in every room, sweeping and making beds. We'd have seen him. Is he mad at you?"

"He must still be in the woods, sulking. I'll take a walk through there in a minute. He'll be in even more trouble for leaving his sister to do his work, which isn't going to go down well."

"Tobias—" She stopped.

When she didn't go on, he said, "I can see it in your face, *Schweschder*. Spit it out."

"Don't be too hard on him. He meant well."

"You mean the chicken? Something must have frightened the poor thing to death to make it fly up there."

"Coyote, probably. You know both of us would have climbed that ladder in a second to rescue it when we were their age."

"The point is, he disobeyed me about going up there at all, even though his motive was *gut*."

"But hasn't he been punished enough? Let Gracie take it out on him if she's upset about having to do his work. Though I don't think she is. She seems to be enjoying it."

"She's a tidy little thing." He sighed. "All right. I'll let it go. But I'm a bit worried that he hasn't shown up all morning. I'm going to take a walk and see if I can find him."

"Want some company?"

"Sure. That bit of forest isn't very big. It won't take us long."

Susanna let Mamm know she'd be back to help clear the *Kaffee* things in thirty minutes, and they set off for the woods.

Tobias used to think that there was nothing more beautiful than the high desert of New Mexico in June, but Montana seemed to have an extra vigor. Maybe because the growing season was so short, even the pine needles seemed more scented, the pink and white of wild roses on the split rail fences more intense. The acres the Zook brothers up the creek had dedicated to hay seemed to have shaken off the setback dealt them by the blizzard and were growing by inches every night.

Maybe that vigor had gotten into his son and, instead of energizing him for work, it had energized the traits that behaved like weeds. It was his job as Benny's father to prune them back until his boy was old enough to learn how to do it himself.

Ah, Lily Anne. If only you were here. Even when the twins were toddlers, before the cancer had clawed its permanent hold inside her, his wife had the gift of calm. No temper tantrum could overcome it—in the moment, at least. She'd lie in his arms later, when they were in bed, and cry at having to discipline the two little beings she loved most in the world. But they never saw her do it in anger or frustration.

Something he'd been guilty of more than once.

"Are you all right?" Susanna looked back, walking ahead of him on the narrow path between the pines that meandered in the direction of the variety store.

"*Ja,*" he said, shaking himself out of memory and into reality. "I was just thinking about how *gut* Lily Anne was with the twins, no matter how loud the tantrums got, or how much *Druwwel* they got into."

"I'm glad they had her during the terrible twos," she said, her gaze swinging between the trunks of the pines in search of her nephew. "At least she had the chance to shape them a little before…"

"Mamm always says the early years are the most important. I'm not sure she's right about their personalities being set by the age of five. Gracie, maybe. Benny is different every day."

"The important things stay the same," she said with a grin. "He hates potato salad just as much now as he ever did when he was smaller."

Tobias had to laugh. "Shall we split up at this fork? He may have gone to the Zook place to console himself with the goats."

"All right. See you at lunch."

The belt of trees ran along the creek, which was still freezing and high with spring runoff. Down by the Inn, it widened just enough to give the fishermen some sport, but up here it was a little deeper and rocks lay at the bottom waiting to surprise unwary paddlers. In the distance, the Zook barn came into view, but the path was obstructed by the trunk of a big old Douglas fir that had to have been sixty feet high. It had snapped off near the base, probably from the weight of eight feet of snowfall during the blizzard, and now lay across the creek, lodged against a cluster of granite boulders on the far bank.

"Looks like my chainsaw is going to get a workout," he said aloud, trying to decide whether it was better to go the long way around by the stump, or climb over it and risk getting pitch all over his hands and work clothes. Mamm and Susanna were old hands at dirt, but pine pitch was a special level of aggravation on wash Mondays.

He was ambling down the length of the trunk toward the jagged stump, when he heard a sound like a goat bleating.

Da-a-a-a-a. Da-a-a-a.

Those blessed goats of Zeke and Willard's! If there was ever a place they shouldn't be, that's where you'd find them. Tobias was half tempted to leave the creature wherever it had got stuck and go up to tell the Zooks to come get it. But that wouldn't be very neighborly. Better to bring the silly animal along. If Benny were getting in the way in the barn, or talking their ears off in the kitchen, maybe a kindness would make up for it.

He rounded the stump and headed back to the rushing creek, where the sound had seemed to come from. But scan both banks as he might, he couldn't see a goat.

Da-a-a-a-a.

There. It almost seemed to come from the water itself, as though—

Ach, neh. Was it a kid born this spring, too small to know its own danger? Had it fallen in the creek upstream and been carried down here, only to be swept into the spiky, thick branches of the fallen fir? A feeling man couldn't walk away now. As for pitch, he was pretty sure he had a can of hand cleaner that Mamm and Susanna could use on his clothes if worse came to worst.

Da-a-a-a-a.

"All right, I'm coming."

He hoisted himself up on the trunk and made his way cautiously down its length to the middle of the creek. The branches were bushy and stuck up every which way, pitch pearling everywhere he grabbed for a handhold.

"Where are you, you hairy rascal?"

"Dat!" came a faint voice from the depths of the branches, some of them submerged in the water.

Tobias felt his heart stop in his chest.

"Dat! Help!"

"Benny!" he shouted, lurching into motion. "Hang on, I'm coming!" He practically tore the branches away, making a path to where the faint voice had come from under the roar of the water. "Where are you?"

"Down ... here."

One last branch cracked and broke under his panicked hands, and there was his son, half submerged, his body pinned by the force of the water against what the fishermen called a *sweeper*—a brushy comb formed by a thick mat of branches. Broken pieces of branch told the tale of the boy's trying to rescue himself and climb up on the thick trunk, but no one his size was going to fight that water and win.

Tobias flung himself to his belly on the trunk, hooked one knee around a branch, and reached down as far as he could. "Grab my hand."

Benny flailed, trying to reach it, but his fingers were already tinged with blue and he couldn't quite make it. Tobias lowered himself further—stretched until it seemed his shoulders would crack—

—and brushed the cold fingers without getting any purchase.

"Listen, son. Can you climb up on anything? A rock? Branch? All I need is four inches and I can pull you up."

"Too—deep—"

One unguarded move and his boy would be dragged under the trunk and pinned there. He would drown before Tobias could get underneath and free him.

"All right. I'm coming in. Don't move."

"Can't."

Tobias tore off his work boots and hat and left them on top of the trunk. Then he went over the side, using branches like a ladder. The last one broke with a *crack!* and into the deep water he went, six feet to the rocky creek bed. The fast, cold water stopped his breath and pushed him into the trunk like a schoolyard bully. But he was no seven-year-old. He was a father filled with equal parts fear and grim determination.

His feet touched a big rock and he braced himself on it—the water only up to his chest now, but far too deep for Benny. He leaned closer and grabbed the boy under the arms. His shirt tore as the branches ripped at him, but Tobias ignored it and backed away, holding him against his chest with one arm and using the other to fend off branches as he fought his way out.

He half swam, half staggered to the bank, where he sloshed up on the grass, gasping not from shortness of breath, but because he was sobbing. "Are—are you hurt? Is anything broken?"

"*N-neh.*" Benny's teeth chattered, his face as white as snowmelt, his lips blue. "I kn-new you would c-come."

"*Ach, mei Sohn.*" Even his tears seemed cold as he chafed Benny's feet and legs. "I've got to get you home."

Holding him against his chest where he could give his boy the most warmth, he barrel-rolled over the fallen trunk of the tree and jogged down the meandering path. It was only a twenty-minute walk between the Inn and the Zook farmhouse, but Tobias did it in ten.

It wasn't until he emerged from the forest and was climbing the slope toward the Inn that he realized he'd run the whole way barefoot, and his boots and hat were still sitting on the fallen fir in the middle of the creek.

&a.

SYLVIA WAS NO STRANGER TO HARD WORK—ON A RANCH, IT was a rare day when a woman could lean on her broom and think, *There. It's done.* Because *done* only meant *until tomorrow.*

A little like God's work in a person's heart, maybe. Every time she thought she might have learned a lesson, it turned out to be only another step on the journey of obedience to *Gott's wille.* Which, she supposed, was only as it should be. A scholar in her first year at the little schoolhouse down the road learned her *Englisch* a letter at a time, then a word at a time, then a sentence at a time, not the other way around. Learning what her heavenly Father wanted of her might come like that, or come in a sudden rush of understanding that was more like a miracle than any human thought process.

Today's work, though, was more like a holiday—her favorite kind. Yesterday, Mamm had mentioned to one of the Zook brothers that she wanted a nice wheel of soft cheese to bake in pastry with herbs and vegetables for lunch tomorrow. Sylvia had seen Mark coming out of the bunkhouse and been quick to volunteer to go and get it. She didn't even bother with hitching up the buggy, because that would take her right into his path. It was a beautiful day and only about two miles over to the Zook place.

After a fast walk that left her red-faced and perspiring, Zeke took one look at her and suggested she take a breather in the shade while he chose a nice cheese and wrapped it up for her. A walk along the creek sounded wonderful, so she took him up on it—after carefully closing and latching the gate behind her, much to the disgust of all the goats and several cows who had their eyes on the hay field.

She hadn't gone far when she found the path blocked by a Douglas fir that had fallen right across it and the creek both. She'd have to let Zeke and Willard know. This was a common shortcut. Besides, goodness knew what would get caught under those branches and—

She squinted. What was sitting up there on the fallen trunk in the middle of the creek?

With a glance both ways to be certain no one was watching curiosity kill the cat, she found a rock tall enough to give her a head start and scrambled up.

Ugh. Pitch. She pulled up her skirts just in time. Then, balancing like a cat on a veranda railing, she walked down the trunk to the strange objects.

"My goodness." She'd recognize those boots anywhere. They'd been made in New Mexico for a man just over six feet, and that straw hat had only been in use for a couple of months and still looked pretty new. "What happened that Tobias left his things here?"

But the rush of the runoff had no answer for her. He wasn't swimming in the freezing water downstream, and when she turned to look on the upstream side, it didn't look good. A lot of broken branches, and a scrap of blue shirting.

Dread pooled in her stomach. He couldn't be pinned under the tree, could he?

"Tobias?" she called. "Can you hear me?"

"*Ja,*" someone said behind her.

With a gasp, she whirled and it was only by the grace of *Gott* that she didn't lose her balance and take a tumble right into the roiling water.

"What are you doing up there?" Tobias stood on the bank,

his hands on his hips and his feet bare. A pair of socks was stuffed in the waistband of his front-fall trousers.

Relief that he wasn't dead under the fallen tree loosened her self-control. "I saw your boots and thought you'd fallen in." She collected them and the hat, then picked her way back along the log to where it crossed the path.

"Careful." He took his belongings from her, jammed the hat on his head, and then seemed to realize that she would need a little help getting down if she didn't want to cover her dress in pitch from backside to knees. He reached up. "Here. Let me help you."

If ever a dream could come true, it was now.

She braced her hands on his warm shoulders and tried not to squeal in joy and alarm as he swung her down. She slid down his chest and his arms tightened around her until she could find her footing on the grassy creek bank.

And for one moment out of time, out of real life, they both stood motionless as she gazed up into his eyes. Blue eyes. And long lashes, dark as his wavy hair. And a funny little slantwise scar that bisected one end of his right eyebrow that she'd never been close enough to see before.

The moment snapped like an elastic. He set her away from him and stepped back, pulling out the socks. "Guess I'd better get my boots on."

Saved by the socks. She flailed for something to say that wasn't, *What happened to give you that scar?* "Why were your boots and hat up there?"

"I found Benny trapped under that tree half an hour ago, and had to jump in after him."

The breath rushed out of her. "Good heavens, the tree didn't fall on him, surely?"

"No, it's been down a few days, looks like." One boot was

on. She only had a minute to keep him talking. "I had to discipline him earlier, when he thought he was in the right, and he set off up the creek to cool down, I guess."

She could imagine what had happened then. "And what *Kind* could resist crossing the creek on a log bridge?"

He nodded, and stood, both boots on. "Lost his footing and went in, and couldn't get out. The current is fierce from the runoff and pinned him in those branches. We'll be lucky if he doesn't have hypothermia—he said he'd been playing in the woods most of the morning, and only fell in about ten minutes before I got there."

Ten minutes was a very long time in glacier melt. "Where is he now?"

"Mamm is seeing to him, with the help of one of the fishermen. He's an RN at some big hospital in Texas."

"*Gott* is looking out for *dei Kind*, then." Words teetered on her tongue. *Oh, go on.* "Have you forgiven each other?"

After a moment of gazing at the creek, which rushed on its way oblivious to human predicaments, he nodded. "Before I got home with him."

"*Ischt gut.*" She paused awkwardly, uncertain whether she ought to say more.

Into the silence, he said, "What are you doing here? Were you on your way to see Mamm?"

She shook her head. "I'm picking up a cheese. It was a warm walk, and Zeke thought a walk by the creek would do me good."

"Your nose is a bit sunburned."

Her hand flew to cover it before a blush spread over the rest of her face. *Wunderbaar.* Now she probably looked like a peeling tomato.

"I'm glad I didn't have to fish you out of the creek, too."

Was that relief, or had he meant to make it sound like it would have been an inconvenience to him? "Why didn't you bring the buggy?"

But there was no way she was about to explain *that* to him. "I'd best be getting back," she said hastily. "I don't want to keep Zeke waiting."

As she walked away, she wasn't certain whether he was watching her go, or if he'd already turned and headed for the Inn. It didn't matter, anyway. He could have caught her doing handstands on that tree trunk and still treated her with that calm courtesy he extended to old and young alike among the *Gmay*.

You're never going to get his attention, Sylvia Keim. She swallowed the lump that rose in her throat. *If you were smart, you'd treat Mark Steiner as more than a friend, the way Mamm and Dat want.*

A chill settled in her stomach, and she'd walked most of the way home in the hot sun with the cheese before it went away.

$$
\text{❧}\quad 5 \quad\text{❧}
$$

THE RN, whose name was Kyle Akimoto, looked up as Tobias leaned in the twins' bedroom. Benny appeared to be sleeping. "How is he?"

"Unchanged since you asked me that—" He checked his watch, which looked as though it could command an entire hospital. "—thirty-two minutes ago. I've got all four of your mother's hot water bottles packed around him, filled with warm water. He's still kind of groggy, though."

"Fighting the water probably took it out of him."

"I think he was in there longer than ten minutes. Lethargy is one of the knock-on effects of hypothermia. It was good you got to him when you did." Kyle must have seen the fear in Tobias's face, because he went on hastily, "Kids recover fast. I went to nursing school in Minnesota, and a kid fell through the ice. He was in there way too long before his friends could get help. And yet he was back at school on Monday."

Mamm joined him in the doorway. "I'll keep the water bottles filled, like you said—warm, not hot. Tobias, you're needed down at the barn. Kyle, you're on vacation. Both of you, leave Benny to me and Susanna."

"But—" Benny was more important than any barn. He was his father. It was his responsibility to do what was necessary. Especially since it was his fault that his son had been so upset he'd done such foolish things.

"No buts," Mamm said firmly. She brought a cup of coffee in with her. "Let the crew know lunch is outside on the veranda. I've already eaten."

Kyle grinned at him and led him outside. "Your mom is right. Everything Benny needs has been done. All he needs now is time to recover."

"Thank you." He gripped the man's hand. "I don't know what we would have done if you hadn't been here. I've never seen a case of hypothermia, even in a New Mexico winter."

"Your instincts were good. You got him out of his wet clothes and into some warm blankets. Resist the urge to chafe his legs and feet, though. You don't want cold blood circulating back to the heart."

"I'll try to remember that next time." Hopefully there wouldn't be a next time, but with Montana, you never knew.

Kyle patted his shoulder and went to make himself a sandwich to take with his rod and creel down to the creek. Tobias slapped something together, but it tasted like sand in his mouth. And that afternoon it was all he could do to follow Noah's instructions. Stand this up. Nail that. Give us a hand with such-and-so. But when the sun sank, the barn was dried in, its roof on and all the siding in place, with neat holes cut where they would install the windows. The doors were hung, too—even the big buggy doors with their wrought-iron trim made by Alden Stolzfus.

"Sim and I will be back tomorrow," Noah told him as he

packed his tools in the wagon. "If you can scare up a fourth man, we can have the staircase up to the bunkhouse built by lunchtime."

"I might be able to convince Seth and Gideon to spend another day here," he said. "I don't want to ask Stephen, even with Susanna as an inducement. They're riding up onto the allotments this week to check on the calves."

Noah nodded at the hierarchy of importance on a ranch. "A couple of nights away?"

"Probably."

"See you in the morning, then. I'll let Seth and Gid know when I get home." Noah grinned. "I want to get your barn wrapped up so I can start on our house and my shop. Much as we love living on the Circle M, Rebecca and I want to be in our own home—and Adam and Kate want a roof over their heads before their wedding, too."

"With the way you all work together, the only question will be whose home will welcome everyone for Christmas dinner."

Noah laughed. "And we all know the answer to that one— your Aendi Naomi's!"

Tobias helped Noah and Simeon hitch up, then watched them roll out in the soft light of the gloaming on their separate ways home. When he walked through the sturdy barn, feeling a quiet satisfaction at how snug it felt already despite its space, he made mental notes of the supplies he'd have to stage before the crew got there tomorrow. It would save their time for more important things, like insulating and sheathing the second story interior, then framing in the dual-pane windows. There would be three windows in the bunkhouse—one on each end and one in the common area, and a small square one in each of the four bedrooms. In what Mamm had taken to calling the *church room*, which other people might call the hayloft, there would be long horizontal windows on each of three sides for light. When it was their turn for church, should that day fall in the winter, neatly covered hay bales would add insulation to the walls.

He ambled out of the south door, which faced the part of the highway that formed Main Street on its way through town, and sank onto what still remained of the lumber pile. The gloaming had deepened into twilight, and from up the slope he could hear someone—one of the lady painters—singing in one of the guest rooms. She clearly possessed more talents than painting, if the quality of her voice was any indication.

> *"When peace like a river attendeth my way*
> *When sorrows like sea-billows roll*
> *Whatever my lot, Thou hast taught me to say*
> *'It is well, it is well with my soul.'"*

As though it had been called up by the old hymn's words, a wave of sorrow rose out of the depths of his being and swamped Tobias every bit as thoroughly as anything made of salt water. He bent at the waist and held his head in his hands, gasping for air and feeling as though he were drowning. Losing Lily Anne, almost losing Benny today, not being able to find steady work to provide his own home for his *Kinner,* not knowing how to keep them safe when he was at work ... all of it tossed his grieving heart from windblown crest to hollow depths.

How could he have gone from loving husband and confident provider to *this* in only a few short years? If it were up to him, he would have picked up both children and gone back into the past, back to when he was happy, and his son looked up at him with trust and joy, not betrayal. When he could walk into the foreman's cabin at any minute of the day and scoop Lily Anne into his arms for a kiss, and hear that bubbling laugh that had so delighted him.

Something grasped his hand and he almost came out of his skin, jerking in a breath that was mostly a sob.

"Dat?" Gracie hung onto his hand as if she might lose him to the undertow. "*Bischt du okay?* Are you crying?"

Gulping down his emotion, he pulled her into his arms. "The hymn," he choked. Well, it wasn't a lie—the hymn had started it all. "It was one of your mamm's favorites."

She listened to the third verse. "What's it called?"

"Can you guess?"

"It Is Well?"

"With My Soul," he finished. "I was missing your mother pretty bad." He seated her on his knee and wrapped both arms around her, burying his nose in her hair. She smelled of wood chips and Susanna's strawberry shampoo. "Have you been picking up nails?"

She nodded, and opened her other hand to show him. "Is Benny going to help me tomorrow?"

He smiled at this reversal of responsibility. "It depends what Kyle says. He thinks he's doing pretty well, though, considering that water is from the glacier. It was ice cold and *Gott* didn't design human bodies to be in it very long."

"Like trout."

"*Ja.* Trout like it cold."

"Benny shouldn't have run away." His daughter relaxed into his arms. "He should have said sorry and gone back to work."

"He did, after I found him. We both said sorry."

"Is that why you were crying? Because you were sorry, and because of Mamm?"

"*Ja*. And because we could have lost him in that creek. That big tree had him trapped pretty good."

"But *Gott* told you to walk up there instead of over to the store. Aendi Susanna said so."

"She might be right."

"She said something else."

He prepared himself for something like, *Aendi Susanna is always right.*

"She said we need a nanny."

A milking goat? "Why?" Weren't chickens enough for his sister?

"Because we need someone to look after us until it's time to go back to school."

His definition of *nanny* underwent an abrupt revision. "I know that Mammi and Aendi Susanna are busy with guests, but among the three of us, we can look after you."

"*I* think we need a nanny," she said firmly. "We've been out of school for almost two weeks and Benny hasn't memorized one single spelling word. And Mammi was supposed to teach me how to sew and she never has. And—"

"*Liebling*, the Inn only just opened a few weeks ago. Give them time to settle in and get used to housekeeping for more people than just us."

"But Mammi says we're booked until way after roundup. Me and Benny will be in *second grade* by then." She made it sound like the end of the millennium. "I want a nanny."

"How does Benny feel about this?" Tobias knew how he himself felt. Like a failure. Again.

"He wants a nanny, too." She twisted around to look up into his face. "We even know who."

Heaven help the poor woman. "Who?" he said, like the barn owl that lived in one of the firs to their left.

But she didn't smile and hoot back. "Sylvia."

This was a picture even more incongruous than the goat. "Sylvia Keim?"

"Can we ask her?"

He needed to nip this in the bud. "I think she probably has enough of her own chores to do on the ranch."

"Bethany and Sharon can do them. That's why they came. To help."

"*Ja*, but it seems to me that if two women needed two more women to help, and you subtract one—"

"Two plus two equals four. Four minus one equals three."

"Well done. That leaves three women having to look after Josiah, and Stephen, and the hands, and the horses, and all the animals, doesn't it?"

"Mamm and Aendi Susanna are two women looking after lots more people than that."

He had to admit that was true. "But there are still the horses and cattle."

"The hands look after them," she said triumphantly.

All right, she'd scored her point. But something more important needed to be said. "We may be a little overwhelmed right now, but we don't push our problems onto someone else to solve. We find a way to do it ourselves that doesn't burden our neighbors."

"Sylvia doesn't think we're a burden."

"Of course she doesn't. But we still need to think of her before ourselves. You know what Mammi says."

"Jesus first, others next, yourself last," she recited. "That spells joy."

"Exactly." He kissed her. "We'll figure it out. It's barely even summer yet, and I bet I could think of a hundred chores to keep the two of you out of trouble."

She slid off his lap and dropped the nails she'd been holding into their metal bucket with a clang. "Chores aren't the same as spelling words. Or sewing. Or learning to drive the pony cart. Or going for ice cream."

Last year, he'd rashly promised he'd teach them to drive the cart. Before they'd had to sell the pony, and moved here, and wound up storing the cart in the barn at the Circle M with all their other possessions. It was still there.

And had he bribed them with ice cream at some point or another, and completely forgotten about it? Were these just two more of the ways he was failing his children?

Gracie released her parting shot. "I bet Sylvia would do all those things with us." And then she ran up the slope as a lamp glimmered to life in her bedroom window.

LIKE MANY OF THE RANCHES IN THE VALLEY, THE KEIMS kept their chickens in the barn instead of in a separate chicken coop, because of the harsh winter weather. Care of the chickens fell to the youngest girl in the family, even if Sylvia was past the point at which people would ever use the word *youngest* or even *girl* to refer to her. Most people didn't refer to her at all, except Mamm and Dat and her relatives. Still, she loved taking care of the flock. It was a mix of older birds who taught the young ones where the best foraging spots were and where to sleep on the roosts The chicks they'd got at the feed store a couple of months ago were half grown and would come into lay in another couple of months. When they started investigating likely hay bales and the nesting boxes, it would be time.

Sylvia counted beaks and then latched the door to the

aviary, soothed by the music the hens made as they settled in for the night. Mamm called it music, anyway. Sylvia had the feeling they were simply warning each other not to get too close.

She wound her way through the calving pens. She'd just said *guder nacht* to a cow that Dat was treating for an infection when the telephone mounted beside the door jangled. One of the chickens sounded the alarm at the unexpected noise and over her shoulder, she told it that everything was all right. At least, she hoped that was the case. Dat and Stephen Kurtz carried cell phones, but here on the home place, the telephone in the barn served its purpose and usually there was someone close enough to answer it.

"Bow K Ranch, Sylvia Keim speaking."

"Is that Josiah's Sylvia?" a familiar voice asked.

"*Ja*, Cousin Abner, it's me. How are you and Delilah keeping? Do you still have snow?"

"I heard from my boys about that little surprise you folks got. Delilah is well, considering. But listen. Talking of little surprises, is your father handy?"

"I'm sorry, he isn't. He and the hands are up on the allotment for a couple of days, checking calves. Can I help somehow? Pass on a message?"

Dat's cousin Abner Troyer and his family lived on a small place near Amity, in the Wet Valley of Colorado. He and his eldest son worked at the buffalo ranch that was the neighborhood's claim to fame. An Amish man named Joshua King was foreman there.

"Ach, this is no kind of news to be giving. I need to ask you all to send those boys of mine home."

Sylvia felt a chill of fear at his tone. "What happened?"

"Well, a cranky buffalo happened, to make a long story

short. He got upset with me for riding a little too close to one of his calves. Charged the horse. I fell off and broke my leg in two places."

"Abner!" Sylvia exclaimed in shock. "That's awful. The buffalo didn't come after you, did it?"

"*Der Herr* was looking out for me, for sure and certain. That beast was satisfied with unhorsing me and scaring my poor paint halfway to the next county. It was just lucky Joshua caught sight of my riderless horse and sent out a search party."

"Good heavens."

"So I'll be laid up for six weeks or more. I need Danny and Pete home to do my job on the buffalo ranch. They have experience, where none of these greenhorns from Ohio and Lancaster County do."

"Oh, my." Sylvia thought fast. "It's too late to ride up into the hills tonight, but we ought to be able to get them on the five p.m. bus from here tomorrow, if someone can meet them in Alamosa the day after."

"I'll take care of that. *Denki*, Sylvia. I appreciate your help."

"You just take care of yourself, Abner. I don't imagine there's anything worse than getting in an argument with a buffalo."

"The buffalo always wins," he agreed. "Give my greetings to your parents."

"And ours to Delilah and the girls. We'll let you know when your boys are on their way."

Sylvia hung up feeling a little breathless. Poor Cousin Abner! Dat had always maintained that cattle were crazy and unpredictable enough for any man, but buffalo were a whole order of magnitude more so. He'd have needling rights over his cousin for years to come.

But when she dialed her father's cell phone number, all she

got was an automated voice saying that her call could not be completed at this time. She tried every hour until well after dark.

Mamm finally stopped her from taking another walk out to the barn. "They must be so far up the mountain nothing but bird calls can reach them. You'll have to ride up there, *Liewi*."

"I was afraid of that." Sylvia sighed. "But someone has to go, so it may as well be me. You'll have to make the bread on your own."

"Nothing I haven't done before, and the girls will help. Go on. Get some rest."

She did, but not until after she'd asked *der Herr* to watch over Cousin Abner, and to direct her and her horse to where his boys were working. The allotment wasn't as big as the one for the Rocking Diamond or the Circle M, but it was still pretty big, and she'd rather not be riding fruitlessly up ridges and down coulees when Abner needed his boys home in such a hurry.

6

BOW K RANCH

Wednesday, June 15

IN THE MORNING, Sylvia pulled her worn jeans on under her dress and rolled her shearling coat up behind the saddle along with a *gut* lunch. "It might take you some time to find them in the high country," Mamm had said as she packed it. "I prayed last night that old Callie here would listen to the still small voice and take you right to them."

Sylvia laughed. "So did I. I'll be home as soon as I can."

Caledonia the mare had been a fine cutting horse in her day. She could still work as well as ever in the home paddocks, but chasing cattle on the allotments for days at a time was beyond her now. Still, she didn't complain as they headed down the road that would intersect the county highway, which took them to the gate they all used to access the allotments in the foothills. The foothills gave way to mountain slopes, and by the time they'd passed the collecting meadows and reached the wide alpine valley that was the main benefit of the Bow K allotment, Sylvia had relaxed and was simply soaking in the beauty all around her.

Summer had come to the little valley and, as though *Gott* were using a paintbrush loaded with every color He had created, it was full of flowers. Lupines, lilies, Indian paintbrush, and mountain heather competed for her attention with bitterroot and glacier lilies. Sylvia smiled, remembering that movie star last year who had outbid Alden Stolzfus for Malena Miller's Glacier Lily quilt. What a fuss that had made! But it had all come out right in the end—the man had sent the quilt back to her and hadn't even asked for his two thousand dollars to be refunded. And she and Alden were courting.

In the distance, she heard the yipping whistle that the hands used to move cattle. Callie swiveled her ears in that direction and Sylvia said, "All right, girl. Let's go see."

When she crested the ridge, she sent up a quick prayer of thanks to the *Gott in Himmel* who cared so much about His children that He had directed her straight to the young men she sought. Stephen Kurtz was riding with them, showing them how to manage the cluster of cattle now that they weren't simply in the home fields. She pulled off her hat and waved it to get his attention, giving the same yipping whistle.

All three rode toward her while the cows lowered their heads and began to graze.

"Sylvia!" Stephen called when he was within earshot. "What brings you up here? Is everything all right?"

"*Ja*, we're all just fine." She gave a sympathetic smile to Pete and Danny and tried to be succinct without being blunt. "But we got a call from your father last night. He's broken a leg tussling with a buffalo—he's all right," she added hastily as horror dawned in their eyes. "It charged his horse, and he fell off. He asked if you both could come home and take over his job on the buffalo ranch while the bone knits."

"But he's okay," Pete asked, as though he wasn't quite reassured.

"He is," she said with a firm nod. "I told him we would get you on the five p.m. bus and he said he'd arrange for someone to meet you in Alamosa tomorrow night."

"That okay with you, boss?" Danny asked Stephen, his horse stepping around hers and gazing down the meadow, as if it sensed his desire to head out right that moment.

"Of course it is," Stephen said. Then he urged his horse closer to hers. "Leaves us shorthanded, though."

That wasn't her business to manage. All she could do was nod in agreement.

"Josiah and Mark are two ridges away, and his cell phone won't work. But I know he'll agree with me. Sylvia, when you get home, can you call Tobias Miller? He's worked with our herd before, and he's the only man I can think of who isn't committed to another outfit and can come at short notice. It's probably too much to hope that he can ride up here this afternoon, but we can really use his help."

She squelched the thrill of joy that tingled through her at having a real reason to talk to Tobias, and schooled her face to its best combination of businesslike and helpful.

"Of course. I'll go over to the Inn as soon as I get back. What will you do if he can't come?"

Stephen made a face. "Make do, I guess. Unless you want to borrow a bedroll from one of these two and give us a hand until Friday afternoon."

She had to laugh at Pete's and Danny's faces. "Don't look like that—it's happened before." She wedged the Stetson she'd found at the Amish school auction a couple of years ago over the blue *Duchly* that covered her hair. "*Kumm mit*, then, boys. I'll show you the way down. *Denki*, Stephen. Any message for the folks at the Inn?"

Was that color flooding his tanned face, or only a bit of sunburn? "Just that we probably won't be back in time for Alden's birthday frolic, but I'll see them all Sunday."

She smiled to herself as she turned Callie for home. It was off Sunday in their district, so he and Susanna would have all day together.

By the time the three of them reached home, it was late afternoon. She left the boys packing while she untacked Callie and turned her out into the pasture, then backed Rhoda the buggy horse between the rails and hitched her up. She was waiting in the yard when they came out, canvas duffels over their shoulders, and after Mamm had kissed them and supplied them with enough food for supper *and* breakfast, Sylvia got them to the station half an hour before the bus was scheduled to come through.

With a wave and a "See you before roundup!" they went inside to buy their tickets, and she clucked to the horse.

Maybe Rhoda could feel her anticipation. Or maybe she simply needed some exercise. But it only took two minutes to reach the Wild Rose Amish Inn, and another minute before Gracie came running up the slope from the barn to greet her as she tied the horse to the rail in the Inn's parking lot.

"Sylvia! What are you doing here?"

"I've just been dropping Pete and Danny at the bus station. Their father needs them at home, so I fetched them down from the allotment and got them into town just in the nick of time."

"Did you come to see Benny?"

"I hope to. But first, I need to deliver a message to your *dat*. Is he down at the barn?"

"*Ja, kumm mit*. We have stairs!"

Gracie grabbed her hand and hurried her down to the construction site, which had come along by leaps and bounds since yesterday. Sure enough, a sturdy staircase now reached up to the second level, faced in hardwood and complete with a railing on both sides for the older folks.

"I was the first one to go up when it was done," Gracie said proudly as she climbed the stairs ahead of Sylvia. "They're putting the windows in now."

The big windows were in, though Sylvia thought they must have had to lift the heavy things up on a pulley through the hay hole. They heard voices in the bunkhouse, and Gracie ran to tell her father she was here.

He came out of one of the bedrooms slapping his gloves together, releasing a small cloud of fine sawdust. "*Guder owed*, Sylvia. What brings you here?"

"A message from Stephen Kurtz. Dat's cousin Abner in Colorado—Pete and Danny's father—broke his leg in a mishap with a buffalo, so the boys are on the bus home."

As though it had been waiting for its cue, the bus rumbled across the bridge and with a roar of its engine, turned south as the zigzag highway made its final zag through the residential district and turned into a proper highway heading south.

Tobias was already ahead of her. "So they're up on the allotment shorthanded."

"Stephen asked if you could take their place. But it's more than just helping until Friday. It's going to be at least six weeks, Abner thinks, before he's up and around again, and able to ride."

Tobias didn't hesitate. "Sure I can. Josiah is a fair man to work for, and of course nothing beats your and your mamm's cooking."

She smiled at the compliment. "You're able to leave the construction for that long?"

"It's dried in. I'll have the last of the windows mounted tonight, and then do the finish work as I'm able in the—" He stopped, and a little of the color faded in his face as he watched his daughter diligently hunting for nails.

"In the what?"

He heaved a sigh and his shoulders slumped. "I can't do it."

Disappointment seemed to clang like an out-of-tune bell in her chest. "Why not?"

He lowered his head, and when he spoke, his voice was quiet. "I need to be here with the children. Benny is having a hard time right now, and Gracie—" A sound in his throat might have been a deprecating laugh. "She thinks we need a nanny. As though her grandmother, aunt, and father aren't enough to look after them."

"I think she's right," came out of Sylvia's mouth without pausing at her brain first.

Tobias stared at her. "You think I'm a bad father?"

"Goodness, no," she said in honest shock. "I think you're the best father in the world. But we all know that Rachel and Susanna have their hands full with the Inn, and it seems to me you're running distracted trying to keep up with the twins as well as manage the construction and do all your other work. A nanny is the perfect solution until school begins after roundup."

"Oh, you think so." He sounded nettled now, as if he thought she and Gracie had planned this out beforehand without even asking first. "And who do you think is going to be that perfect solution with no notice? Any *Maedscher* who isn't already working is too young."

Sylvia had made up her mind the moment he'd said the word *nanny*. Her heart was galloping like a runaway mustang as she teetered on the brink of the bravest, craziest thing she'd ever done.

Then she looked into his tired eyes and took the leap. "Will I do?"

***

"You are so smart." From his nest of blankets, Benny grinned at Gracie and offered her the other half of the cookie he'd been hoarding for a bednight snack. "How did you pull it off?"

"I'm not sure," Gracie confessed, and bit into her half. "Why is it that things we're not supposed to have always taste so *gut*?"

"Mammi says it's the *Deifel*, but I don't think he has time for stuff like cookies," Benny said frankly. "I can't believe Dat agreed to it."

"I might have had just a *liiiiitle* bit to do with it. Remember I found him last night, crying on the lumber pile?"

"I never would have believed it, except for his eyes were all red when he came in to say good night."

"Well, I might have said out loud about the pony cart, and about the ice cream we never got, and a couple of other things."

"Ouch. None of those were his fault."

"Except the ice cream."

"I bet we get it now. Sylvia likes ice cream."

She nodded. "And not homemade, either. From the ice

cream shop in town. They have great big waffle cones. And *sprinkles*."

"So do we get to go to the Bow K tomorrow?" Benny narrowed his eyes. "I'm fine now. I got up and went down to the creek today, while you and Aendi were cleaning. Until Mammi found me. She was kinda mad."

"I don't think so. Sylvia is coming here tomorrow, and staying over until Dat comes down the mountain."

"I can talk Sylvia into letting me be normal. Kyle says one more day, but I bet she'll let me go out tomorrow."

"She will," Gracie said with confidence. "Our plan is working perfect. Nothing can go wrong. Right?"

Her brother swallowed the last precious bite of the cookie. The peanut butter thumbprint ones with the jam in the middle were his favorites. And he only got a teensy bit of jam on the sheet. Easy to lick off.

"Right," he said, and when he grinned at her, you'd never believe he'd come *this close* to death only yesterday.

They had all the crumbs wiped off their faces and hands and onto the sheets when Dat came in to hear their prayers and say *guder nacht*. "Noah is bringing Mars with him on his way to his property. He's going to stake out his house with yellow string," he said as he kissed first Gracie, then Benny. "It will be *gut* to ride Mars again. They've treated him well at the Circle M."

"Even better to have a barn to keep him in." Gracie liked how the kiss stayed on her cheek. "Maybe even when you get back."

Dat smiled, but it didn't quite reach his eyes. "The work on the barn will go slower with me over at the Keim place. We might not get the horses for another month. But we'll worry about that another day. For now, I had to promise to take twenty-seven messages up the mountain to Stephen before Aendi Susanna will let me out of the house." When Benny looked at him in disbelief, Dat smiled for real. "Well, it felt like twenty-seven." He got up. "You two be good for Sylvia, you hear? She'll be sleeping in Susanna's room while I'm gone, and Aendi in mine."

"*Ja, Dat.*"

His eyes softened as his fond gaze moved from Gracie to Benny. "And you stay in bed one more day, until Kyle says you can get up."

"*Ja, Dat.*"

"I love you. See you Friday night."

"Love you, Dat," they chorused. The door closed gently behind him.

"Gracie?" Benny whispered, in case Dat was still outside.

"What?"

"Are we really going to be good?"

"*Ja*, I think we'd better be. If we're bad, the whole plan goes down the drain. We want her to be our *mamm*, don't we?"

Benny snuggled down. He didn't hate his comfy bed as much as he let on. "Maybe just a little bit bad. So we're not being deceitful. She ought to know what she's getting."

Gracie considered this. He had a point. "Okay. Maybe just a little bit. Now, go to sleep."

7

WILD ROSE AMISH INN

Friday afternoon, June 17

THE TWINS WERE WASHING their hands in the family bathroom when Rachel stopped Sylvia in the hallway. "Are you sure you don't mind taking them to this frolic of Alden's? There won't be many *Kinner* that young, or many *Youngie* so—" She stopped herself just in time.

But Sylvia wasn't offended. She'd been thinking the same. "Not many *Youngie* in my age group," she finished charitably. "It's all right, Rachel. Really. It's probably all over the district by now that I'm looking after them, so if people see them, they'll expect me."

"Susanna should take them," Rachel sighed. "But oh my goodness, I had no idea that Friday evenings would be like rush hour around here. We're discovering that ninety percent of the people like to come on Fridays. As though it makes any difference what day it is when they're in the river fishing."

"But it might make a difference if they have to ask for vacation days," Sylvia pointed out. "Best to start with a weekend, *nix?*"

"I suppose." She glanced into the guest parlor. "I just heard doors slamming out there. We're expecting a family of five, with three kids under ten."

"Maybe some playmates for the twins."

"*Englisch* playmates? Goodness only knows what trouble they could get into. I'll try to discourage it if it comes up." And she hurried to the front door to greet her guests.

Gracie and Benny ran out in clean clothes, their hands and faces shining. "You look tidy enough for church," she said with a smile. "I just have to get the cake we made from the fridge."

Carrying the layer cake in a tall plastic holder with a handle that kept it closed, she smiled shyly at the family unloading in their luggage.

"Mom! Look at the Amish kids!" the tallest one exclaimed. "I want a hat like that."

"We'll be here for a week," their mother said. "We can get one later. Come on, each of you deals with your own suitcase."

"But mine's heavy," the middle boy moaned.

"You're the one who insisted on bringing the video games to a place that doesn't have electricity," his father informed him.

The kid watched Sylvia and the twins cross the Inn's rustic little bridge to Creekside Lane and then finally pulled out the handle of his suitcase and dragged it inside after him.

"What's a video game?" Gracie wanted to know.

"Something to do with television?" Sylvia guessed. "They have them at the library, but I have no idea how they work. Come on, let's see if any of your guests are fishing under the big bridge."

They weren't, but downstream a little, Benny waved at a man in the hip waders. "He said he and his wife stayed at the old Inn after their wedding when they were young. But she died."

"Poor man," Sylvia said. "I hope his memories are happy."

And then Rose Stolzfus's little house came into view, and from the number of Amish *Youngie* and *Kinner* standing and gabbing, or running around getting into everything, even if a person didn't know the house, they'd know there was a frolic going on.

"Off you go," Sylvia said with a laugh. "I can see the Eicher kids on the trampoline—you'll both be in Matthew's grade in September."

She took the cake into the kitchen, where Rose was just taking a big square pan of bubbling macaroni and cheese out of the oven.

"Hi, Sylvia," she said over her shoulder. "I know this isn't the right season for macaroni, but Alden loves it. He gets all his favorites for his birthday. Malena has been out back slow-roasting ribs all day."

"It all smells *wunderbaar*. Where do you want this cake? It's my gingerbread pear cake—Mamm's special birthday recipe."

"Ooh, I hope I get a big piece of that. There's a dessert table outside. Better not take that cover off just yet—wait till the bugs die down."

Outside, in the backyard that extended into a small orchard of tiny, stunted trees, two volleyball nets had been set up, with games already in progress. Alden and redheaded Malena Miller played on the same side, of course, though they were getting plenty of teasing about it. To her astonishment, Mark Steiner was playing at the other net. He spiked the ball and the girls on the sidelines cheered as it bounced off the ground inches from Calvin Yoder's cupped hands.

Sylvia's stomach did a flip. Did that mean that Dat and his crew were down from the allotment? That Tobias might come over? Or did it just mean that Mark had ridden ahead and everyone was still at the Bow K?

Well, she wasn't about to ask him. She hadn't forgotten she was supposed to ride home with him, though she'd have to explain she had the twins with her and they were only going to the Inn. With an internal smile, she figured he might just rescind the offer. If she was lucky.

She found Rebecca King and Sara Miller talking together, while Sara's little Nathan toddled around on the grass with Deborah Miller, who was only a few months younger yet was Nathan's aunt. The two of them were looking at interesting bugs and showing the young *Fraas* a leaf here and a dandelion there.

Both young women were younger than Sylvia, but she had known them all their lives. And there was a sweetness in the two *Kinner* playing together that caught at her throat.

Me too, Lord? Some day?

"They're so adorable," she said to Sara. "I can see a family resemblance, too, can't you?"

"The blond hair is a dead giveaway," said Rebecca, laughing. "Mammi Miller was as blond as could be. I hope I'm like her— blond until I'm sixty, and then pure white after."

"I hope so, too," Sylvia said. "I was a towhead when I was these little ones' age, and then it seemed to darken. Mamm says Dat was the same way."

"Are they still up on the allotment?" Rebecca asked. "Noah took Tobias's horse over to him the day before yesterday."

Sylvia lifted one shoulder. "I don't know. I would have thought so, but Mark Steiner was with them, and he's here."

"Only just," Rebecca said. "He came about five minutes before you did. In a buggy." She and Sara exchanged a look. "I wonder who he's taking home?"

Sylvia bent to catch Nathan as he charged straight for her, and turned him in the opposite direction. At a toddling run, he headed for Deborah, tripped on a tussock, and fell flat, nose to nose with a gopher. With a shriek, he hollered for his mother, who caught him up and settled him on her hip. Bless the child for being a distraction and a bit of comedy, too. Because every rancher has strong opinions about gophers, and people who own hay farms do, too. Which meant the subject of Mark Steiner didn't come up again, and Sylvia breathed easier.

The parade of hot dishes for supper ended the volleyball game, and after a silent grace, the clatter of plates and cutlery and serving spoons was enough to scare the deer into the hills. Alden beamed as he invited Malena to precede him in the food line. When Sylvia got there, the array of food was almost intimidating.

"Some spread, *nix?*" Mark Steiner was in the line going down the other side of the table. "Nothing like a potluck."

She had to agree. Along with a ham, glistening with pineapple and honey and half carved into slices, there was the pan of macaroni and cheese, a big bowl of taco salad, and an equally big bowl of Chinese chicken salad. An eclectic mix, to be sure, but when the menu includes a person's favorites, anything goes. Add to that half a dozen kinds of pickles, heaps of potato buns, and the whole dessert table waiting beyond, and Sylvia knew she'd have to pace herself or the twins would have to trundle her home in a wheelbarrow.

She spotted Gracie and Benny in the line with the Eicher

children, Benny's eyes as big as saucers at all the food. It was *gut* that they'd made friends. Seeing another child at church was a different thing than seeing them in a setting like this. She had no doubt that they'd be jumping in the hayloft of the little barn before long, and getting up to who knew what mischief. But since they were eating with the other family, she could relax and eat the delicious supper.

Folding chairs had been set up, but Sylvia left those for any older women who had come, and settled to the grass nearby. She had just taken a big bite of macaroni and cheese when Mark Steiner, her cousins Bethany and Sharon, and Alden's two sisters, Beth and Julie, settled around her in a cluster.

Was she expected to play chaperone for these girls while they flirted with Mark? With a sigh, she concentrated on her supper.

"We thought you'd be gone till tomorrow night," Sharon said to Mark. "Did you find all the calves?"

"All thirty-seven," he said. "They hadn't gone far—most of them got hung up in the valley with all the flowers."

"I can't blame them," Sylvia couldn't resist saying. "Every year it's like *Gott* takes special care in making that valley beautiful. I hate to leave it, too."

"She had to go up to tell our hands that they had to go home to Colorado," Sharon explained to the Stolzfus girls.

"Their father got trampled by a buffalo," Bethany added.

"He didn't get *trampled*," Sylvia said hastily. "His horse threw him when the buffalo charged."

"I bet it was close to getting trampled," Bethany said.

"But we don't want to embroider the story," Sylvia said. "Too much of that and before you know it, poor Abner will have been killed and the boys had to go home for the funeral."

"Who was killed?" David Yoder sat down and made himself comfortable on the grass.

"See what I mean?" Sylvia said, laughing.

He eyed her. "Doesn't seem like a laughing matter."

Oh, for goodness sake. He was so stuffy and literal. "No one was killed. We're just having the next best thing to a game of telephone. Two of our hands had to go home, is all. A horse threw their father and he broke his leg."

"Tobias Miller came up to take their places," Mark said, shoveling in ham and taco salad in equal proportions. "I'm glad he was free or we'd have had to stay up there another day."

But was Tobias here? She waited for Mark to say so, but just like a man, he put his stomach first above all.

"Sylvia!" Gracie and Benny, plates in hand, plunked themselves down on either side of her, and Mark had to move over or have a twin practically in his lap.

"Well, hi. I thought you'd eat supper with the Eichers."

"We wanted to eat with you."

"Awww," Sharon and Bethany chorused. "Do you like having Sylvia for your nanny?" Bethany went on.

"Mm-hm." Benny's mouth was full.

"She's going to take us for ice cream," Gracie said, mouth equally full.

"Not today," Sylvia said hastily. "I think there's plenty of dessert made by kind hands on that table over there."

"Cake!" Benny said with something akin to rapture.

"I thought you had hypothermia," Julie said to him. "That was a narrow escape."

"I thawed," Benny said around a piece of ham.

"Don't talk with your mouth full," David advised him.

Benny gave a mighty swallow. "If I didn't, I wouldn't be able to talk at all."

"That doesn't seem like a bad thing. We were having a conversation before you came and interrupted us."

Enough was enough. "David," Sylvia said steadily, "if Benny is to be chastised, I will do it. *Denki*."

"But you didn't."

"That doesn't mean you have to put your oar in," Mark said. "Leave the kid alone."

Offended, David got up with his plate and walked away to sit with another group.

"Now you'll have to apologize," Beth Stolzfus warned him.

"What a stick in the mud he is," her sister said. "I pity the girl who marries him."

Sylvia bit down on the urge to say that, like a dose of salts, he'd already been through all the prospects in the valley, the most recent being the bishop's daughter. Gossip wasn't a good look for anyone, especially a woman who was supposed to be setting an example for the children in her charge.

"I'll apologize, all right," Mark said easily, "when Yoder apologizes for stepping on Sylvia's toes."

"He stepped on your toes?" Gracie said, aghast. "When?"

"Not my actual toes. He means David overstepped," Sylvia said. "It's not his job to tell you not to talk with your mouth full. It's my job, and I guess I need some more practice."

"I think you're doing great," Mark told her.

"It's only been a day. Not really enough time to say that," she told him, with a smile for the twins.

"The day isn't over yet." Mark grinned.

Gracie leaned against Sylvia's arm, and frowned at Mark. Then she looked up. "We're not really bad, are we?"

"Of course not." She kissed the top of the little girl's bucket-shaped *Kapp*.

"That's not what Tobias says," Mark teased. "Something about a chicken?"

And just like that, the easy, fun atmosphere evaporated from the little circle. Both children addressed themselves to their plates.

Sylvia frowned at Mark. What did that mean? What chicken? The new one that Gracie had introduced her to yesterday?

"Have you heard from Pete and Danny, Sharon?" she asked at last. "Were they able to get to Alamosa tonight?"

"They might have called after we left to come here," Sharon said. "Mark, did Onkel Josiah say if you'd have to go back up the mountain next week?"

He shook his head, apparently unaware that his last remarks had put a chill in the air. "Nope, we'll be working closer to home. All the irrigation ditches have to be checked, and apparently a cow came home scratched up. That probably means a fence is down somewhere, so we'll be heading out to look. Oh, and speaking of Tobias, he'll be bunking with us. No point in him riding back and forth and tiring out his horse before his day's work even starts."

Tobias bunking at the Bow K! This was news to Sylvia. "When did that come about?"

"On the ride home," Mark replied. To the twins, he said, "Think you'll manage without your *dat* for the rest of the summer?"

Benny's dark eyebrows wrinkled into a frown. "Why is he staying at your ranch?"

"Because he's working there until Pete and Danny come back."

Sylvia spoke gently to Benny, through her own surprise.

"He's got to do the work of two hands, but I know he'll do it well, don't you?"

"I don't want him to go all the way out there." Gracie put down her fork and tears welled in her eyes. "He's our *dat*. He lives with us."

Sylvia shot Mark a *now look what you've done* glare. If anyone was to have broken this news to the twins, it ought to have been Tobias. Not chucked at them by a man they hardly knew, in a casual remark like an afterthought.

"We'll talk it over with your father when we see him," she said now. "Are you done with your plate?"

While the twins joined the Eicher horde at the dessert table, she collected the plates and took them into the kitchen to start the dishes.

But Rose and Malena, Kate Weaver, and Ruby Wengerd shooed her out again. "Never mind the dishes now. We're just putting the candles on Alden's birthday cake."

There was going to be enough cake to have the whole valley bouncing off the walls. Maybe she'd better keep a closer eye on the twins, and make sure they kept it to just one piece.

Rose and her helpers came out with the cake and all its lit candles, singing Happy Birthday while everyone joined in. Then it was a bit of a free-for-all as pieces went around. Mark Steiner, she noticed, sidled up to her gingerbread cake and snagged not one piece, but two. And to her surprise, he brought them over and offered her one.

"*Denki*, but that's the one I made," she told him. "I'll just have a piece of the birthday cake. Chocolate is always a hit."

"I know this is the one you made. That's why I took two pieces. No man in his right mind would turn down a piece of your cake."

She resisted the urge to roll her eyes like a fourteen-year-old. "Enjoy."

"Oh, I will. Say, what was that all about earlier? The thing about the chicken? You'd think I'd butchered it or something."

There was no way that she could give him details of Tobias's business. She didn't even know what had happened, really. "I'm not sure, but I think somehow the chicken and Benny's nearly drowning in the creek were tied up together. You saw how quiet they got."

He chuckled. "I bet that doesn't happen often with those two."

"They're *gut Kinner*. They make mistakes, but they always mean well. There is no malice or unkindness in either of them."

"Sounds like you know them pretty well, for a family that just moved here this year."

"They went to school in the west district for a couple of months," she said. "I helped out with rides and whatnot, and got to know them a little."

"Well, better you should have your own family than look after other people's."

She had to take two deep breaths before she could speak. "Wouldn't that be nice? But it takes two to arrange that, I think."

"It sure does. You haven't forgotten about my giving you a ride home, have you?"

No, sadly. "Things have changed since the other day, Mark. Why make the horse walk less than half a mile when the twins and I can walk it in just a few minutes?"

He stared at her, then started on the second piece of cake. "What does that mean? Walk where?"

"To the Wild Rose Amish Inn. I've been staying there to look after them while Tobias was up the mountain."

"And now he's back."

"And staying on the Bow K, apparently."

"Then I'll take you home."

"What about the twins?"

"What about them? You take them back to their grandmother and aunt, and I'll pick you up and take you back to the Bow K. It's better that way, anyhow. Too many people will make too much of it if they see us leaving together from here."

She was already shaking her head. "I can't do that. Tobias will tell me what he wants his children to do, and I'll abide by it. For now, I'm sorry that plans didn't work out, but it's just not a *gut* time."

"Well, what about Sunday? There's a singing at Yoders'. How about I give you a ride home then?"

She chuckled, but it was more in exasperation than anything. "Mark, I can't give you an answer. Yoders' is right next door to the Inn. If I'm still there, it's a two-minute walk through the woods."

He gazed at her, clearly perplexed. "You are a difficult woman to be friends with."

"I hope we already are friends. You've been working for us for a while."

"I meant a special friend."

Oh. "Mark, I—"

"A man doesn't usually just come out and state his intentions with a girl this early, but clearly you're not like other girls."

"I'm not a girl," she said gently.

"You know what I mean. Woman."

Yes, she knew. A woman older than he, halfway in love with another man. But she couldn't exactly say that out loud.

"Let's play it by ear," she suggested at last. Vague, maybe, but it was the best she could do. "It's been a crazy week. Things should settle down soon and we can see where we are."

He seemed to cheer up. With a sinking feeling, she realized that while she might have meant *we* as in the Inn family and the ranch family, he might have thought she meant *we* as in the two of them.

Oh dear.

But when he offered to fetch her a piece of birthday cake, she used the twins as an excuse, and hurried away into the soft twilight to find them.

❧ 8 ☙

Saturday, June 18

Tobias came out of the bathroom and stopped dead the instant before he collided with Sylvia, who was washed and dressed in light green and apparently on her way into the kitchen. "Oops, sorry."

She gave him some space like a nervous grasshopper, touching her *Kapp* as though to make sure she hadn't forgotten to pin it on. "When did you get in?"

"Last night, late. I stayed for supper with your folks and talked a little business."

She nodded, her lashes lowered. "I do the books and look after the hands' pay, so that means Dat will have some notes for me." She looked behind him, though the corridor was empty. "If Susanna was using your room, where did you sleep?"

"Not upstairs in a guest room, that's for sure. We've got a full house. And since it wouldn't do the Inn's reputation any good if I stretched out on the guests' sofa, I bunked on the one back here."

A smile glimmered on her mouth, making her look more like the reliable Sylvia he knew. "True enough. Come and have some coffee. We need to talk a little about the twins before they wake up."

Oh, boy. That didn't sound *gut*.

He combed his wet hair, fastened the rest of the snaps on his shirt, and tucked it in. Socks and cleaned boots made him feel as though he could take on the day. Coffee would help with that, too.

He found two cups steaming on the table outside on the little patio. The sun wasn't up yet, but it was going to be warm, the sky a pale lemon darkening into blue. He took a moment to check that his cutting horse was doing all right on the slope down to the barn. Luckily, the half acre or so was fenced on three sides, and the animal was too well trained go into unfamiliar woods without a rider. He grazed quietly near Mamm's fenced garden, clearly an optimist where young, leafy vegetables were concerned.

Sylvia joined him with a little pitcher of cream in one hand and the sugarbowl in the other. She offered him the bowl, poured a dollop in her own cup, and sat opposite him.

"How do you remember what I take in my coffee?"

She lifted one shoulder in a shrug. "Mark, Danny, and Pete all take theirs black. Stephen takes both. You take it black with sugar. So this season, I only have to remember two of you."

"That orderly mind of yours." He took a sip. Delicious. "So, what do you have to tell me about my *Kinner*? Be blunt. I can take it."

Her lashes flicked up in surprise. "Are you expecting bad news? I have to disappoint you—other than eating one more piece of cake last night than they should have, they've been their usual happy selves. They weren't the only ones eating more cake than was *gut* for them, for sure and certain."

"Was it a *gut* party?"

"It was a feast, and there was volleyball, and one of the Petersheim kids fell out of an apple tree, and one of the Eicher kids got too close to the *Englisch* neighbor's German Shepherd and nearly got bit." She smiled. "You know. A normal Amish birthday party."

"And here you were, looking after my *Kinner* instead of having fun yourself."

"We had plenty of fun. I discovered I haven't lost my talent for Simon Says, and neither has your cousin-to-be Kate Weaver. We had those kids plenty *verhuddelt*, I must say." She tilted her chin proudly.

"So if they weren't giving you trouble, what did you need to talk about?"

She took a sip of coffee, then another, as though gathering her thoughts. How strange it was to be sitting opposite each other. Just the two of them. He was used to their eating at the big Keim dining table, full of raucous hands and everyone talking a mile a minute. Now, it reminded him of quiet mornings in his little kitchen in the foreman's cabin on the Four Winds Ranch, just him and Lily Anne B.C.—Before Children —talking over the day to come and making plans. Not big ones, not life-changing ones, but little ones. What he'd be doing that day with his brothers. Whether it was wash day or bread day or baking day. Whether they'd eat at the big house that evening or in their own home.

"Tobias..."

He blinked and came back to himself. "Sorry. I was wool-gathering."

"Drink some more coffee," she advised, and had another

sip herself. "Mark told me yesterday that you planned to bunk at the Bow K instead of riding back and forth from here. It didn't go over very well with the twins. So I hoped to hear from you how it should all be managed."

He'd had plenty of time to think over the logistics of it all on the way down the mountain. "Your father and I did some talking, and it's his opinion that it makes more sense for me to live in the bunkhouse for the summer, considering emergencies and coyotes and workload. You know, all the things we have to deal with."

"That's what Mark said, too. No point tiring your horse before you even get to work, he said."

It finally sank in. "Mark was at Alden's birthday party?"

She nodded. "He didn't know I was staying at the Inn with the twins. He—we—well, he was supposed to take me home, but that didn't work out."

She had his full attention now. "Mark Steiner wanted to take you home? Is that why he was in such an all-fired hurry to get down the mountain?"

"I don't know," she said from the depths of her cup. "All I know is what I told him. That I couldn't. The twins and I walked home the long way, past the Zook brothers' place and down the creek. I figured it would be *gut* to let them wear off some of that sugar before they went to bed."

"Did it work?"

"Mm-hm. It only took one story to put them out. But getting back to what you'd like to do..."

He'd like to drop some hints to Stephen about giving Mark more work.

When he didn't go on right away, she said, "I think the children want to be near you. Gracie was pretty upset that you'd be so far away all summer. I know it's only four miles, but that's a long way to walk when you're seven."

"And you probably don't want to live here all summer, either," he said. "Not when you've got your own work at home. There's only one thing to do. If it's all right with your mother, bring the twins to the Bow K."

"To the Bow K," she repeated. "That's quite an adjustment for them."

"They've been there before, and not just for church. They'll be with you, and I can be with them in the evenings and for breakfast."

She sat back, as though this idea had never occurred to her. "I'll have to check with my parents. We have a spare room, but it only has one bed."

"Benny can sleep in the bunkhouse with me, and if you have a cot, Gracie can sleep with you."

"Benny would love that. There are twin beds in my room, from when I used to share with my sister." Then her lashes fell and color flooded her cheeks.

She was so modest. Tobias had heard that the Keims had been pretty strict with their children, though you wouldn't know it from the adoration and spoiling the grandchildren got. So probably his bringing up the subject of beds—a man who wasn't a family member—had just embarrassed Sylvia to death.

"We don't need to do anything right this moment," he said, doing his best to put her at ease. "I'll call your folks and tell them you agree with the plan. If they agree, too, I'll let you know."

"All right." She half rose, then sat down again. "Goodness. I'd better think about what they'll need to take with them. I should have brought a pen and paper out here."

A muffled clash of pans sounded in the kitchen, and female voices.

"That's Mamm and Susanna, making breakfast. How many fishermen like to be out early?"

"About half of them," she said, sounding distracted.

He took pity on her. "You go ahead. I'm going to finish this. It's *gut Kaffee*."

"*Denki*. I was up first, so I made it." She rose, collecting the cream and sugar on her way past.

Tobias relaxed into what were probably the last few minutes of leisure time he was likely to get, other than Sunday. He listened to the sound of breakfast being assembled in his mother's kitchen. The murmur of Sylvia's voice added to hers and Susanna's. A kind of harmony lay in the three voices, kept low so as not to disturb anyone who wasn't already up.

He drained his coffee and hoped there was more inside. Sylvia made a *gut* cup.

❧

COULD THIS MORNING GET ANY MORE DISTURBING?

Sylvia put her few overnight things in the small gym bag she'd come to the Inn with, and took a moment in the quiet of Susanna's room to breathe. In her wildest dreams, she'd never imagined coming face to face with Tobias this morning, fresh out of the shower, his shirt half done up, his hair wet, and smelling of soap and warm skin. Her knees had gone weak at the sight of him, and she'd skittered away, averting her eyes lest he see that all she wanted to do was throw herself at him and feel his mouth on hers.

She knew perfectly well what would have happened if she'd been that crazy. He would be shocked, then say he only thought of her as his sister in Christ, and he would never, ever speak to her again—not with the ease of their few minutes outside with coffee. He'd make sure they were never alone, and she wouldn't put it past him to make encouraging hints to Mark Steiner, too.

Mark Steiner. She bit back a groan.

The man himself was waiting outside with the Keim buggy, looking pleased as punch at doing her such a favor. Mark had somehow convinced her father that she and the twins needed to be collected today, not tomorrow, when Sunday visits had people out in their buggies and her parents would have been happy to come by for a visit, see the progress on the barn, and take them home with them.

"*Kumm mit*, you two," she said, leaving the bedroom spotless and tidy, her bag in one hand and her purse over her shoulder. "Mark is waiting for us."

The twins ran out, dragging the little rolling suitcases they'd used during the family's move to Montana, and carrying their pillows under their arms.

"Here are some snacks," Rachel said, handing Sylvia a plastic container of cookies and raspberry coconut squares, while Susanna tucked a chocolate bar into the outside pocket of each suitcase.

"Rachel, we're not getting on a train," Sylvia said with a laugh. "Only driving four miles."

"It's a taste of home." Her gaze followed the twins as they ran out to the waiting buggy, suitcases bumping along behind them. When she turned back to Sylvia, tears glimmered in her eyes. "It occurred to me this morning that we've never been separated for more than a few days. It's going to take me a little minute to get used to the idea of six weeks."

"We'll be back often," Sylvia assured her. "I'm sure we've forgotten something, so it may be as soon as tomorrow."

Rachel nodded, then straightened her shoulders. She picked up Tobias's duffel, which he'd packed the night before, and went out to put it in the back of the buggy and kiss her grandchildren good-bye. A flurry of hugs and farewells concealed the fact that Susanna's eyes were damp, too. Then Sylvia was obliged to climb in next to Mark and off they went, looking for all the world like a family of four.

And wasn't Mark aware of it—too aware, if that erect posture and little smile meant anything. Was it too much to hope that no one would see them on four miles of road? She supposed there was one blessing—Tobias had ridden out earlier to begin work with Stephen. At least he wouldn't see this—this fake approximation of a family that she was quite sure Mark had been counting on to speak for him.

"Nice day for a drive, *nix*?"

You'd think he'd read her mind. "It is," she agreed. "So nice that I wonder how you managed to get out of this morning's work. Riding fence, wasn't it? To find where that cow broke through?"

"Tobias is there," he said easily. "Not like it's challenging work for the whole crew. Kate's pretty excited that you're coming home, and Josiah is glad to have one hand that can do the work of two boys."

"Our *dat*," Benny said from the rear bench.

"Or me," he agreed quickly, over his shoulder.

"Or Stephen," Gracie added loyally, considering Stephen would be her *Onkel* one day.

"How many hands would that make, if three can each do the work of two men?" Sylvia asked gently, to turn the conversation. Mark was looking a little nettled.

The two of them made a game of counting their own hands and hers, too. "Six!" Benny said triumphantly.

"That's right," she told them. "Josiah is getting quite a deal."

"Do I still have to do my spelling words at the Bow K?" Benny wanted to know.

"*Ja*, you do," she said firmly. "You don't want to be the only one in second grade who doesn't know them, do you?"

Reluctantly, he supposed not. "I wish I could do arithmetic instead. Gracie is *gut* at spelling words. I hate spelling."

"We don't hate, even something we don't care for," she reminded him.

"I don't like spelling."

"I don't either," Mark said unexpectedly. "The letters get crossed up when I look at them. Numbers, too. Maybe I should join you at homework time. Get some practice."

"I think two is enough for someone like me, who isn't a teacher," Sylvia said awkwardly. The last thing she wanted was to be seated at the table with him instead of Tobias, who Susanna said took an interest in his children's progress at school.

"Look, there's Zeke!" Benny waved at him out the open back window. "*Guder mariye,* Zeke!"

There went her hope of no one's seeing them, and it was only the first mile.

Three miles later, Mark had smiled and waved at every buggy on the road, every Amish person running an errand, and even one or two ranchers in the fields. He was doing it on purpose, she just knew it, and the word would be all over the valley by suppertime that he was courting her.

Add this to her having so foolishly told Tobias that Mark was supposed to have driven her home from the party, and she'd be walled off from him in a ring of speculation just as surely as if she and Mark really were dating.

She heaved a sigh of relief when they finally arrived at the ranch and the children could jump out. They had both seen Tobias, and truth be told, half her attention was on those distant figures two fields away, riding fence, as well. But the twins deserved her whole attention. So, while Mark drove the buggy into the barn to unhitch the horse, she took them into the house.

"Here are our little boarders!" Mamm exclaimed, bending to kiss them and giving Sylvia a hug of greeting. "Are you hungry? Do you want something to eat?"

"*Neh, denki*," Gracie said shyly, as Sharon and Bethany cooed over them. "Thank you for having us to stay."

"You're most welcome. It's the only sensible thing to do—and we're so grateful your father was able to help us. I hope you'll think of the Bow K as your home until you go to your real one after roundup. Sylvia, why don't you get them settled while your cousins and I get a snack ready for the hands. Maybe you and the twins would like to take some coffee and cake out to their father and Stephen?"

Sylvia's heart gave a thump at the sound of his name. Goodness. She was going to have to control her emotions now that they were living on the same place. She couldn't very well jump and blush every time someone mentioned him, or be caught daydreaming about his silhouette in the distance. The last thing she wanted was for her family to know that she had feelings for him—feelings that weren't returned.

But such was the fate of spinsters, *nix*?

A short while later, the twins climbed the fence into the first field, then took the basket and the Thermos she passed through the rails before she climbed it herself. They had only gone a little distance through the flowers and grass of the five-acre field before they heard the beat of hooves behind them.

Mark rode up with a grin. "Want me to carry those, Sylvia? I promise we won't eat everything before you get there."

They may as well turn around and go back to the house, in that case. But Gracie beat her to it. "*Neh, denki*. We'll take them to our *dat*."

"You can carry them back, though." Benny was clearly finding the basket heavy, so Sylvia traded it for the Thermos flask.

Mark laughed as though the child had made a joke. "Not me. I've got work to do. See you."

Gracie frowned after him as he rode to join Tobias and Stephen. "I don't like him."

"He's a *gut* man, Gracie," Sylvia said gently. "And your elder. *And* your brother in Christ."

"He didn't even ask if we wanted to come here today. It's off Sunday tomorrow, and I wanted to work on my puzzle."

"He thought he was helping. You can't fault a person for that. If you did, they'd never offer their help again."

"I suppose," she said reluctantly.

"Do *you* like him?" Benny wanted to know.

"He's all right," Sylvia said carefully. "But I don't think he's staying over winter. It's hard to really get to know someone when they're only here until autumn."

"I think he likes *you*."

Sylvia felt a niggle of apprehension. Since when were seven-year-olds so perceptive? "I hope most of the *Gmay* do."

"I mean he *likes* you. You said he wanted to give you a ride home. Aendi Susanna says that means a man wants to court you."

"Well, I don't want to court him," Sylvia blurted. They

were almost within earshot of Tobias and Stephen. "Hush, now. No more personal remarks. It's rude."

"But—"

"Gracie, I mean it. No more talk about Mark. It's gossip, and the Lord can't abide a gossip."

"It's not gossip when it's about *you*," the little girl muttered.

"Gracie!"

Thankfully, their father dismounted, walked out to them, and swung her up in his arms. "Look who's here!" He hugged them both as though it had been five days, not five hours since he'd seen them last.

"We brought *Kaffee*, Dat!" they chorused, and Sylvia's tension melted as their father helped them take the goodies out of the basket. They handed out cups, and Sylvia poured coffee. No cream or sugar this time, but the hands never expected that. They appreciated the midmorning snack no matter what it was or how it came.

With a gulp of coffee, Stephen washed down a piece of coffee cake with apple topping. "Is everyone at the Inn planning to be home tomorrow?"

"He means is Aendi Susanna going to be there," Gracie confided to her father.

"Of course Aendi Susanna is going to be there," Tobias said to Stephen with a grin.

"How else are they going to plan their wedding if she's out visiting other people?" Mark teased.

"He hasn't asked her!" Gracie sounded scandalized.

"How do you know?" Mark asked her. "You're only a little kid."

Oh dear, this was the absolute wrong thing to say. Sylvia had only known Gracie since March, but even she knew that no child liked to be dismissed just for being a child.

Gracie glanced at Sylvia, as if checking that the rule about making personal remarks still held. Sylvia smiled with what she hoped was encouragement.

But Tobias stepped in. "I think we'd know if you had," he said mildly to Stephen. "Whenever it happens, our whole family will be pretty happy, won't we, kids?"

Benny and Gracie nodded.

"They'll be glad to see you at the Inn, Stephen," Sylvia added. "The barn is looking really *gut* now."

"What about the interior?" Stephen asked.

And then they were off about the next stage of the construction that Tobias planned for his day off the following Saturday.

"Maybe you could bring the twins over," he said to Sylvia, startling her in the middle of a discussion of stalls for horses.

"Well—why—you could take them in the buggy, Tobias. My parents won't mind."

"But we'd stay the night, and go to church with Mamm and Susanna in the morning. It's not far to the Benjamin Yoders— we'll likely walk. I'm pretty sure your parents have a better use for their buggy than lending it out to us."

"Oh. *Ja*, of course. Whatever you think best." Words came out of her mouth while her mind flashed ahead to spending Saturday at the Inn, maybe joining the twins to help on the construction site, maybe taking them swimming in the gentler end of the creek—downstream from any fishermen so they wouldn't scare the trout.

Mark, who was standing next to her drinking his coffee, bumped her arm. "What would you think if I came along?" For a moment, she couldn't parse what he meant. The question must have been in her eyes, because he went on, "You and I could do something fun after you drop off the kids. Go for a hike at that park up at the west end of the valley. Or just go window shopping in town. I've never had a chance to yet. Only been in to get feed."

To buy herself some time to find an answer, she said, "You haven't been to Yoder's Variety Store? Or Bell's Books and Candles? Or Rose Garden Quilts? Not even Alden's smithy?"

"*Neh.*" He laughed. "And a cowboy doesn't usually find himself in a quilt store. But if you wanted to, I'd go with you."

"If I went to the Inn, I'd be watching the children. I don't expect to have a day off just because Tobias does."

"You should have a day off sometime," he pointed out. "Why shouldn't it be Saturday, when the *Kinner* are with their family?"

There was no answer to that question that she wanted to give. "Let me think it over. I've only just started the job. I'd hate to upset the apple cart by asking for too much too soon."

"Nobody is going to begrudge you a day to yourself, Sylvia."

"I know. Will you have another cup of coffee?"

"*Neh.* Time to get to work. I've already had more time off today than both these guys. I need to make it up."

To her vast relief, he handed her his empty cup and mounted his horse, then rode off down the fence line as though his single mission in life was to find that break. She and the twins packed the leftover goodies, wrapping paper, and cups and flask in the basket, waved at Stephen and Tobias, and headed back across the fields.

"I'm glad we can go home on Saturday," Gracie said, practically skipping.

"That's a whole week away," Benny said. "I want to explore around here. Can we, Sylvia?"

"Of course. By yourselves, or with me?"

"By ourselves!"

"You can start by taking your gear up to the bunkhouse," she suggested. "That's the first thing all our hands do. You'll be bunking with your father and Mark. Stephen has his own room, since he's the foreman, but the hands have bunks."

"I don't have to sleep next to Mark, do I?" Benny did not look pleased at the prospect.

"That's up to your father. You can explore anywhere on the home place. Just don't go near the bull's field, or out on the road. The eighteen-wheelers use it sometimes, and it's not safe."

"Okay." Benny grinned at his sister. "Last one down is a rotten egg."

✾ *9* ✾

BOW K RANCH

Sunday, June 19

EVEN THOUGH THERE was no church service, there was something sweet about an off Sunday, Tobias always thought. The bare minimum of ranch work had already been looked after—feeding animals and chickens, making sure the horses in the home paddock were all present and accounted for, checking the irrigation gates. By the time they gathered for a late breakfast at seven, the sun had risen over the peaks and it was so warm that Josiah predicted they'd have a thunderstorm that afternoon. When Mark pointed out there wasn't a single cloud in the wide Montana sky, Josiah only shrugged and dug into his plate of scrambled eggs oozing with cheese and spinach.

Tobias smiled to himself as he buttered a biscuit for Gracie, then helped Benny to a couple of slices of bacon.

"How did you sleep in the bunkhouse, Benny?" Kathryn Keim asked, passing the biscuits to Sylvia.

"*Gut*," he said through a mouthful of bacon. Remembering

his manners, he swallowed and went on, "I like it up there. From the door, I can see all the way down the lane."

"And he doesn't snore," Mark reported, slathering raspberry jam on a biscuit.

"You do," Benny pointed out.

"Do I?" Tobias asked curiously, when Mark chose not to reply.

"*Ja.* But not very loud." He looked over at Sylvia. "He sounds like when our dog used to snore. Just little snores, when he was warm and safe."

Sylvia looked as though she was trying not to laugh. "I'm glad your father feels warm and safe in the bunkhouse. Tell them what it was like during the blizzard, Mark."

He lifted a shoulder. "Pete and Danny and me, we thought we'd stay in for the duration, to look after the animals. We've got a store of food up there. Until the snow got so deep the second day that it wasn't safe. We gave the stock double rations and then dug our way up to the house."

"Same," Stephen said. "I won't forget that experience in a hurry."

"At least you got a girlfriend out of it," Mark said with a grin. He spread the hand that wasn't holding the biscuit. "Unlike me. All I got was Pete and Danny."

Everyone laughed. Then Josiah said, "Guess you'll have to try harder."

Out of the corner of his eye, Tobias saw poor Sylvia blushing, her eyes down as she ate steadily. It wasn't really fair to tease her when Mark was so clearly the last man she'd ever choose. But what had gone on when everyone was housebound, that there was no lack of trying? Was that blush embarrassment, or pleasure at a special memory?

The biscuit turned dry in his mouth, and Tobias gulped his coffee to wash it down.

After the breakfast dishes had been washed and put away, he took the twins by the hand into the living room. The family settled into chairs and the sofa. Josiah said, "Right about this moment, our brothers and sisters in the other district are singing the *Lob Lied*. So we will join them in singing it, too. Mark, will you be our *Vorsinger*?"

Flushing with embarrassment at being singled out, Mark began the opening notes to the hymn they all knew by heart, which was always the second hymn in any Amish service. Sometimes his mouth ran away with him, but when it came to singing, Tobias had to admit Mark led it well. When the last long notes died away, Josiah asked Tobias to pray.

Startled, he paused a moment to collect his thoughts. But in truth, he had a lot to be thankful for. A *gut* place to work. Provision for his *Kinner*. And loving hands to help all three of them. Once he began with that, it wasn't so hard to lift up his voice to the Lord.

When he concluded, Josiah said "Amen," and opened the Bible—not the big one that had been in the family for generations, and sat on the hewn mantel in the place of honor, but one small enough for a child's lap.

"Next Sunday we'll hear about Luke twelve and thirteen. Little Joe calls these chapters *bringing in the hay*," Josiah said, "but I think Jesus is teaching us all the ways our spirit can grow by taking lessons from the things that grow in the earth."

Josiah began with the parable of the rich man who tore down his barns to build greater, only to find out, once his barns were stuffed with produce, that God required his soul that night. Then he handed the Bible to Sharon, who was sitting next to him. The book progressed around the room, each reading as many verses as they chose, until it reached Gracie.

"And he said also to the people," she read slowly, beginning where Tobias's finger lay on the page, "When ye see a cloud rise out of the west—" She stopped.

"Straightway," Tobias prompted.

"Straightway ye say, There cometh a shower; and so it is. And when ye see the south wind blow, ye say, There will be heat; and it cometh to pass. Ye—"

"Hypocrites."

"—hypocrites, ye can—"

"Discern."

"—discern the face of the sky and of the earth; but how is it that ye do not discern this time?"

Benny struggled with the next verses, but Tobias patiently helped him with the hard words. Sylvia was the last to read, her quiet voice somehow turning the verses into a kind of music.

"Then said he, Unto what is the kingdom of God like? and whereunto shall I resemble it? It is like a grain of mustard seed, which a man took, and cast into his garden; and it grew, and waxed a great tree; and the fowls of the air lodged in the branches of it."

At that moment, a raven flapped past the living room window, croaking, and the twins grinned at each other in delight.

"*Gott* is listening," Benny whispered to Tobias.

"He is always listening," Tobias whispered back. "This is how He hears our prayers, even when we don't have the strength to speak them aloud."

And it struck him, even as Josiah closed in prayer, that Sylvia was like that mustard seed. Insignificant, nearly invisible, yet in some ways her branches were spread to provide for small living things like his children, giving them shade and a place to rest, yet firm enough to correct them when they went astray.

Thank You, mei Vater, for prompting her to help me when I was at the end of my rope. Thank You for her gentleness that disguises a firm grip on right and wrong. He lifted his head as Josiah rose to put the Bible away and Kathryn and Sylvia went into the kitchen together. *And I pray that You would find her a gut husband some day, Lord. Someone better for her than Mark Steiner.*

WHILE THERE WAS NOTHING MORE LOVELY THAN A JUNE evening in the Siksika, that didn't usually include a heatwave like today's. The verses little Gracie had read that morning were turning out to be prophetic—a single grey cloud had appeared over the horizon at lunchtime, and had quickly grown into a sky full of rumpled, dirty rain clouds. And despite the fact that they provided shade, they did nothing to lessen the heat. In fact, Sylvia was pretty sure the closed-in feeling over the valley was making it worse.

She adjusted her sweating, sticky self next to Bethany on the rear bench of the Keim buggy. At least she'd managed to avoid the front passenger seat. Sharon was only too happy to fill that place, and she chatted with Mark almost exclusively while he tossed the occasional observation about the heat over his shoulder as he drove the three of them to Yoders'.

There were one or two shadows of a different kind on this late afternoon. Tobias had taken the twins in the spring wagon to the Inn to collect a few items that had been forgotten—like Sunday shoes and a clean *Kapp* for Gracie—and to visit with

Rachel Miller and Luke Hertzler. It was a toss-up whether Susanna and Stephen would be at Yoders', at home, or out on a drive by themselves. Sylvia thought they might go to the singing, since it was just a short walk. But then, opportunities for them to be alone were few and far between, and who wouldn't want to take a drive and find a little privacy?

Mind you, they'd have to use a closed buggy. She could smell rain in the air. Thank goodness the Miller barn was dried in. And the hay farms had taken off the first crop.

How had she let herself be talked into going to singing, anyhow? She hardly went anymore. It was too uncomfortable being the senior single when her buddy bunch of the same age, who might have offered companionship and a place to blend in, had one by one all married and either moved away or had homes of their own.

At around the three-mile mark, the route took them past the little one-room schoolhouse where the twins would be going in September. A quarter mile farther on was the intersection with Creekside Lane, on the far corner of which was the Zook dairy. Sylvia could see Zeke and Willard herding the goats to the barn, with varying degrees of success.

And here was the parcel that Rachel Miller had deeded over to Noah and Rebecca King, a nine days' wonder that had been the subject of speculation and consternation around many a dinner table in the valley not so long ago. But Sylvia figured Rachel was in the right. She could do as she liked with the odd-shaped little parcel, which was now sporting wooden stakes with yellow string running from one to the next. But mostly, having a carpentry shop and house builder smack in the middle of the community was a smart and providential thing. Noah would have more business than he knew what to do with, and Sylvia had overheard Rebecca say at the barn raising that she wouldn't mind learning how to make cheese and yogurt herself. Come the day when Zeke and Willard got too old to chase goats and lift heavy cheeses down for customers, it might be a useful thing if someone in the *Gmay* knew their secrets, wouldn't it?

A flash of lightning illuminated the interior of the buggy as though Dat had shone his big box flashlight inside, and before Sylvia could even say, "One thousand and one," thunder detonated right over their heads.

Sharon screamed and covered her ears. Mark fought the horse, Rhoda, who shied and then bounced up and down on her front feet as though she would either bolt or rear. Before she could do either, another bolt of lightning lit up the sky, thunder crashed so loudly Sylvia couldn't even hear Sharon scream, and the skies opened up as though *Gott* had dumped a lake-sized bucket of water into the valley.

Mark flung the reins at Sharon and leaped out of the buggy. He grabbed the horse's halter, clearly intending to calm it. But the horse, startled at the sudden appearance of a man out of the downpour, reared up, bunched its hindquarters, and leaped into motion.

"Sharon!" Sylvia screamed. "Grab the reins!"

But Sharon was nearly hysterical with fear, and when lightning flashed again and the thunder deafened them all, she curled into a ball on the seat, holding her hands to her ears and moaning.

Sylvia flung herself onto the front seat, gabbling a prayer half to *der Herr* and half to the panicked horse. "Rhoda!" she shouted, snatching at the reins. "Rhoda, whoa!" But the Keim buggy horse, normally so well trained and obedient, had the bit in her teeth now, and she wasn't about to listen to anything so unreasonable as a command to stop when the whole world was coming down on her head.

It was all Sylvia could do to haul the reins in close and hope to goodness an *Englisch* car didn't decide to come down Creekside Lane looking for a shortcut.

Not that they could. In less time than it took to cover a quarter mile at a gallop, the graded road had turned into a morass of mud. The windscreen took what Rhoda kicked up and globs of mud ran down in rivulets of rain, completely blinding Sylvia. She hauled the horse in tighter.

The buggy's rear wheels slewed to the right. "Rhoda!" Sylvia cried. "Stop! Whoa!"

Now they were in the deeper mud of the wayside. Beyond it was a short but steep bank and the rushing, glacially cold creek where Benny had nearly perished. She had to control the horse or they'd be flung through the blackberry bushes and overturned down the bank.

She hauled on the left rein and Rhoda jerked toward the middle of the road. But only a jerk. One of the rails of the slewing buggy tapped her flank and, panicked, she jerked the other way, her hooves clattering as she tried to find purchase in the slippery mud. They were still rolling—the mud grabbed the right side wheels while the left were free, turning them toward the creek. The roar of the rushing water, full of rocks and deadly cold, seemed to fill Sylvia's ears as the left front wheel came off the ground.

From somewhere, Sylvia thought she heard a shout, but it could have been Sharon, gabbling prayers into her knees while Bethany hung onto the rear bench for dear life, her face white as bone and her eyes wild.

Rhoda stiffened her forelegs and put her head down. The

reins pulled tight, wrapped around Sylvia's hands as they were. Rhoda reared up and the right wheels of the buggy stuck fast in the mud of the bank, halting their blind flight with a jerk. Rhoda dropped to her feet and, dazed, through the mud-covered windshield Sylvia saw something move. A second shadow. A horse?

She didn't dare release the reins. She didn't dare move lest the buggy tip and everything—buggy, passengers, horse—go crashing down the bank. She was suspended in time and cacophonous noise, teetering on the knife's edge of certain catastrophic injury.

The buggy jerked and Bethany screamed, throwing her arms around Sylvia and falling to the floor, clinging like a limpet. Sylvia nearly went over backward, saved only by her grip on the reins. Her hands were going to be frozen to this leather for a week.

It took a minute to realize they were moving. Forward. Out of the mud, inch by inch, Rhoda's hooves clattering on the muddy road but finding purchase at last.

Slowly, slowly forward. Five steps. Six.

Was poor Rhoda back in charge of her wits? Was the horse saving them and herself?

Sylvia unwound one wrap of rein length from around her hands, giving the horse a little slack. She could still see nothing, though the rain pounded down and lightning flashed, farther away now, heading south toward the Siksika River.

She should halt her and get out. But she could not move, simply sat in the driver's seat, feeling as though she were in a dream, while the horse, jittery but steady, walked down the road.

They turned right. The wheels rumbled over a bridge.

The highway. They were turning onto the highway and she

couldn't see where they were going! "Rhoda!" she shouted again. "Whoa!"

Obediently, the animal came to a halt.

Sylvia had the presence of mind to wrap the reins around the brake lever before she fell out the driver's side.

Literally fell. Because her legs had lost the ability to hold her up.

"Whoops!" said a voice as familiar as her own. A pair of strong arms caught her. "Careful there. You've had a bad scare."

Stunned, speechless, Sylvia gawked at the parking lot of the Wild Rose Amish Inn, then up at Tobias Miller. His short beard was slick with rain and mud, his hat was gone, his brown hair soaked flat against his skull. She had never been so glad to see anyone in her life.

She put both her stiff, sore hands on either side of his beautiful face, yanked his head down, and kissed him full on the mouth.

❧ 10 ❧

TOBIAS STOOD in the rain like a fence post, shocked to the core of his being. His lips still felt the press of Sylvia's, his face the cold imprint of her hands. But he did not move, not even to lift his hands to set her away from him.

She did that herself.

She walked around the mud-spattered buggy and pulled her cousins out of it, both girls wiping tears and rain from their faces. All three were drenched to the skin in less time than it took to cross the parking lot to the Inn.

"Are they all right?" The voice startled him into movement. Mark Steiner appeared on the other side of the horse. "We'd better unhitch her, *ja*? Time to break in that new barn?"

He wasn't sure his mind could hold anything more than what Sylvia had just done. But he forced himself to answer one question at a time. "I think the girls are okay. *Ja*, I'll take the horse down there. The stalls are built and the curry box is in. No hay yet."

No point trying to stay dry—it was like being in a cold shower. And just as well. The rain had already sluiced Sylvia's kiss from his mouth, and by the time he and Mark had unhitched the horse and he was leading her down the slope, Tobias had almost begun to wonder if he'd dreamed the whole thing. Hearing the screams up the road, running to help, and seeing the out-of-control horse nearly take them over the side into the creek ... that was vivid enough. Storms rolled in and out of the Siksika all the time. Horses got spooked.

But Sylvia Keim never, ever allowed herself to lose control or do anything the least bit controversial.

Had he been the only witness?

Had it even happened?

Shaking his head, he took off Rhoda's harness and draped it over the wall of the stall. Then he took a towel and rubbed the horse down as much as he could before he curried her. Half the mud from her feet and legs was already making a trail to the barn door. Barns and dirt were a fact of life. He was just thankful they had somewhere to put the poor animal while she recovered from her experience. And, to his relief, she didn't seem to be cut or even bruised.

She whickered, as though to inquire about the chances of oats.

"Sorry, girl. We're not quite in business down here yet. You'll have to wait until you get home. But maybe I can scrounge up some grass for you."

When he'd found her some feed and returned to the house, he saw that most of the mud had already been scoured from the Keim buggy by the rain. And was the pounding downpour lightening just a little? A blessing if it was.

He went inside, toeing off his filthy boots in the mud room next to Mark's. The man had hung his hat on the peg Tobias usually used, so he tossed his own on top of a coat. Then he went inside, where the lady painters were seated on the sofa with cups of tea, paging through what looked like a book of landscapes. They glanced up, smiling.

"Hallo, Tobias. Everyone is in the back, drying off. Some storm, eh?"

"That it is. Just enough to remind us of who's in charge, I guess."

"I'm just glad we decided to stay in and paint on the verandah," the younger one said. "All our blocks of paper would have been soaked to mush in this."

He pushed through the door to the family side of the inn to find Mark and the three young women telling Mamm and Luke all about their near accident. Luke sat on the sofa with the twins, wide-eyed, on either side of him, while Mamm bustled around the kitchen putting coffee on and cutting big pieces of what looked like applesauce cake.

Sylvia was patting her arms and shoulders dry with a dishtowel. "Was it you who guided poor Rhoda in?" she asked him as he closed the door behind him. "We were one thunderclap away from going down the bank."

"*Ja*, I saw you were in trouble, so I caught the horse and covered her eyes. She calmed down enough that I could lead her into the parking lot."

"That's what I tried to do, and she bolted," Mark said. "There's a sight I hope never to see again—a buggy going down the road with no one at the reins."

"Sylvia was," Bethany said.

He went on as though he hadn't heard. "I took off at a run but couldn't catch up until they got stuck in the mud."

Sylvia flexed one hand. "I might have bruises tomorrow from hauling on the reins so hard. *Denkes*, Tobias. You just might have saved the three of us."

She hadn't looked directly at him once since he'd come in. Maybe he hadn't dreamed that kiss after all.

Mark looked disappointed, as if she ought to be thanking *him*. For what? Abandoning the buggy and letting a panicked horse bolt with it?

"I'm just glad the still, small voice prompted me to investigate the noise," he said. "Someone must have screamed."

"Probably me," Sharon said in a small voice very unlike her own. "Storms frighten me worse than anything."

"Or me," Bethany said, dabbing at her sister's arms with her towel.

"Or me," Sylvia added. "I wonder how many of the *Youngie* got caught out in it?"

"We were late," Mark pointed out. "So maybe not that many. When you girls are dry enough, we can always walk over."

Sylvia went to the parlor window to look out, and Tobias could swear she made a face. But whether it was the thought of going to the singing or out in the weather, he couldn't tell. "It's still raining."

"But there's a little bit of sky." Benny slid off the sofa to point. "See? Some blue again, in the south."

She smiled down at him. "All we need is a rainbow, *nix*? And *Gott* will have kept his promise never to allow a flood like Noah's again."

He grinned and sang the first line of the Noah song, making her laugh.

"Well, I'm game to walk over to Yoders'," Mark said. "We'll go by the highway. We'd probably sink up to our ankles if we took the shortcut through the woods."

"What, all four of us go to singing soaking wet?" Sylvia

asked him. "You three go. I've had enough excitement for one day. I'll hitch a ride home with someone."

Sharon and Bethany begged her to come, but she was adamant.

Then Mark went over to stand beside her. He was clearly trying to convince her, but his voice was pitched too low for Tobias to hear over the twins singing the Noah song to each other from opposite sides of Luke's relaxed body. Luke may even have been humming along.

Mamm brought in the coffee, and milk for the twins, and Sylvia murmured one last something to Mark. She detached herself from him and went into the kitchen.

Tobias pushed himself off the wall by the door and joined her. "Sylvia—"

"I'll take the cake in if you bring the forks," she said.

"All right. But Sylvia—out there—"

Holding the tray of luscious pieces of applesauce cake with maple walnut frosting, she swerved around him like a hockey player avoiding a check, and went into the sitting room. He had no choice but to do as she said and follow.

He wasn't going to give up. He wasn't looking for an apology for that moment of madness out in the parking lot, but he couldn't just ignore it, either. Any man could see that she had been incredibly upset. A compassionate man would make certain she was all right. And a prudent man would find a gentle way to let her know in the clearest terms that it couldn't happen again.

Because whatever lay in her heart—whatever feelings she thought she harbored for him—well, they just weren't possible.

If Tobias knew one thing about himself, it was that he was a one-woman man. He and Lily Anne had been soulmates, brought together by *Gott* to share a rewarding life filled with work, laughter, children, and quiet times where they thanked Him together for His blessings. A life like that could never be repeated somewhere else, with someone else. It had been so perfect that, in the way this old world had of balancing the scales, he should not have been surprised when it all came to an end.

Dat had died unexpectedly. Lily Anne hadn't gone in to have the pain in her abdomen checked out until the cancer had reached stage four. Mamm had sold the ranch that Dat had intended his sons should run. And now Tobias was left without wife, home, or future.

He was just marking time here in the Siksika Valley. Praying daily but not seeing a way forward. Lurching from job to job without any of them becoming steady and permanent. It had been sheer misfortune that had brought him the job at the Bow K, and sheer luck that Sylvia's pay as their nanny was so reasonable because she would be living at home, not having to pay room and board at the Inn.

Someone put a helping of cake into his hands and he obediently took a bite. Mamm's talent with applesauce cake had not lessened over the years. It was still his favorite; he'd asked for it for his birthday as a boy. But tonight he'd lost his taste for it.

Sylvia was drinking coffee with hers, not taking part in the conversation around her. Maybe regretting the strange impulse that made people do crazy things immediately after surviving a crisis.

That kiss had been crazy, for sure and certain.

Not unpleasant. But definitely crazy.

❧

IF SHE COULDN'T GET AWAY TO COLLECT HERSELF SOON, Sylvia was either going to break down or run screaming into the road. She was coming to the end of her rope. Everyone thought she was so calm, so capable, when most of the time it was more a case of biting back what she really wanted to say, or preventing herself from doing what she wanted to do.

That moment with Tobias? She had simply lost control. She couldn't have prevented that kiss unless someone had tied her to the buggy.

And now, like most impulses, there was nothing to do but forget it had happened and hope that Tobias would forget it, too. It sounded like he wanted to talk about it, but good grief, she knew exactly what he would say.

I'll never get over losing my wife.

We can only ever be friends.

You're so good with the children, you'll make some man a wonderful wife. Mark, for instance.

Sylvia put down her fork, the delicious cake turning to sand in her mouth, and washed it down with another mouthful of coffee. It was hot, and the cake went down sideways, and she coughed and spat coffee every which way. Mortified, she grabbed the damp towel from Bethany's lap and covered her mouth, then fled to the kitchen.

Better yet, out the back door.

It was still raining, but not as hard as before. Sunny, the chicken who had adopted the family, peered out of the hen-sized coop door, then ducked back in. The speckled hen, nameless as yet, had a look at Sylvia and did the same. Ah well, she was already damp—she crossed the patio and slid the little door closed for the night, then seated herself on the verandah step, under the old-fashioned overhang of the roof.

She could only stay a minute before someone—Mark,

probably, heaven forbid—came looking for her. They'd wonder what was the matter, other than coming inches from death. But she couldn't very well tell them.

I kissed Tobias Miller and now he thinks I'm not only crazy, but shameless, too.

A door closed at the front of the house, and she heard voices chattering in the parking lot. A couple of minutes later, Mark and her cousins appeared on foot around the corner below the house, where Creekside Lane met the highway. Sharon caught sight of her and waved, and she waved back.

What miracle had made them take her seriously and go without her? In a moment they were out of sight, and for the first time since they'd left the ranch, Sylvia could breathe.

Until the kitchen door opened. She froze, praying it wasn't Tobias coming out to give her The Speech. She couldn't bear it. She braced herself to run.

But it was only Rachel.

Inhaling, Sylvia did her best to relax. Maybe she was only coming out to put the chickens in. But no, Rachel climbed past the step Sylvia was sitting on and indicated the pair of lawn chairs on the south facing side of the verandah. "More comfortable. Less damp."

They might be only webbing and aluminum, but at least they were dry. And the southern sky was clearing, turning pink, the far reaches of the still obscured sunset farther around to the west.

Rachel gazed at it. "Skies here are different from New Mexico, but I'm coming to like them."

"They certainly have their surprises."

Rachel chuckled. "Blizzards, monsoons ... what next? A tornado?"

"Don't say that out loud."

"Too late. But maybe you'd like to tell me about a storm of a different kind. A quieter kind, but no less harmful. Are you all right?"

Her tone was so gentle that Sylvia's eyes filled with tears. "Ach, I'm fine. We all had a bad fright, but it's over now."

"Is it what made you lose your head and kiss my son?"

Sylvia's mind went blank from shock. Her lungs seemed to collapse and for a moment, she couldn't get her breath.

"I heard the buggy cross the bridge. I took the lady painters their pot of tea and happened to glance out the window. It's been a long time since I saw Tobias that ... what was the word one of our guests used last week? *Gobsmacked*." She chuckled again—more like a giggle this time. "It was good for him. Maybe it'll shake something loose."

"Wha—what?" Sylvia couldn't have heard correctly.

"I mean that my boy has been carrying such a heavy load these last few years. It's crushed down his ability to feel, I think." As though Sylvia had spoken, she waved a hand. "Oh, I don't mean he can't feel love for his *Kinner* or his family, because of course he does, and shows it every day. But I think of Benny in the creek. How I hear Tobias weeping late at night. He feels he's a bad father."

Sylvia sucked in a breath and filled her lungs. "He asked me that. If I thought he was a bad father. It shocked me. He's a wonderful father. How could he think he isn't?"

"It's hard for him to see that in himself. Hard to feel the *gut* feelings ... joy in a child's laugh or a rose blooming for the first time after years of neglect. Interest in the silly things the chickens do or the twins say. Sometimes Gracie will tell him a joke and he doesn't even smile." She sighed. "The load is crushing him."

"What ... can we do?" Sylvia knew what she would do. Pray

without ceasing for his burden to be lifted. She half expected Rachel to say exactly that.

"Are you interested in Mark?"

She was so surprised that she blurted, "Of course not."

"You're sure?"

Where was this going? Why were they talking about Mark? "*Ja*, certain sure. My parents wish I wasn't. They've got it all planned out—Stephen marries Susanna and stays on as foreman, I marry Mark and Dat trains him to take over the ranch. I know he sees the two of us running it together some day." She tried to ease the note of resentment in her tone. "I'm the only one of his *Kinner* who wants to stay on. My siblings have all married and moved away. But if his plan includes Mark ... I can't."

"You can't get with the plan ... because you care for Tobias."

Heat prickled into her face in the way that told Sylvia she was ugly blushing. As fair as she was, she turned red as a ripe tomato, and there was nothing she could do about it but wait for the tide to recede. She couldn't even deny what Rachel had just said.

Because to deny it would be a lie.

Rachel reached over and laid a heavy hand on her knee. The kind of hand that got your attention. *"Gut,"* she whispered fiercely, giving Sylvia's knee a shake. "You love him with everything you've got. You're exactly what he needs, and he's buried so deep in his own grief and his own self that he can't even see it."

For the second time, Sylvia doubted her own ears. But she must have heard right. Her knee was beginning to hurt.

As though she'd just realized it, Rachel released her. "I mean it. Susanna has known for weeks."

"Known? How could she? I haven't—"

"When a woman loves, *Liewi*, it's very hard to hide it. Ask me how I know." She smiled, thinking maybe of Luke, still holding the fort inside. "I just wanted *you* to know that both of us are on your side. And so are the twins, if I'm not mistaken."

Almost all of Tobias's family wanted her, Sylvia Keim, to marry him? She was finally able to meet Rachel's eyes, her own wide with astonishment. "The twins, too?"

A number of strange incidents and odd things they said fell suddenly into place.

"I see you've realized what they've been up to," Rachel said. "As misguided and mistaken as their efforts have been, their hearts are in the right place. Did you know they found a wedding ring in the creek bed a few days ago?"

"Neh." Her mind was still whirling, rebuilding her memories of the days since the barn raising in this new light.

"When Benny was recovering, I was sitting with him one night. He showed it to me and asked if he should give it to his father."

"A wedding ring? But we don't wear such things. Especially not the men."

"He knows that. But a ring in the hand is worth two in the creek, evidently. If Tobias couldn't muster the courage to ask you to marry him, Benny wanted to know if he could ask you to be his Mamm. A ring would seal the deal, *nix*?"

Sylvia's face heated again as one hand went to her lips. Not for the first time this afternoon, she was torn between tears and laughter.

"I told him it didn't work that way, and we ought to find the owner somehow. But it goes to show how they feel about you."

Sylvia had to take a moment before the lump in her throat would let her speak. "But how—what—?" she managed.

"Gracie told Tobias she wanted you for her nanny. That was why it was all arranged."

Sylvia stared, feeling her own heart bumping in her chest. "Gracie did?"

"So that was a start. For the rest ... prayer," Rachel said simply.

"I've *been* praying."

"*Pour out thine heart like water before the face of the Lord,*" Rachel murmured, sensitive enough not to look at the blushing, emotional mess Sylvia was becoming. "*Der Herr* already knows the cry of our hearts. He knows already what we need. What He's looking for is willingness for the way His hand will move on us. It may not be the way we think."

Sylvia gazed out in the same direction—across the field, across the roofs and gardens on the far side of the highway, to the mountains beyond the Siksika River that lifted their snow-covered tops to catch the last gleaming of the sun.

"*I will lift up mine eyes to the hills, from whence cometh my help,*" she whispered. How often she'd done that, growing up in this valley.

But ... were her eyes really on that source of help? Because where the eyes went, the feet followed. Was that the error she'd been making? She had been praying without ceasing for Tobias to notice her. And in one way, he had, thanks to Gracie and Benny. But there was a world of difference between noticing an employee and noticing a woman as a possible wife.

Is that where I've gone wrong, Lord? Please help me to be willing for whatever You hold in Your hand for me. If my place is to be single and to look after my parents in their old age, help me to do that with all the love in my heart. If my place is—

—not Mark, Lord, please not Mark—

She took a breath.

If my place is by Mark's side and Your will is that I give up my dreams of Tobias, then grant me the willingness to accept it, to love it, even, knowing that Your will is greater than mine, and Your purposes are always for the good of the Kingdom.

And if, oh, if—

Another breath.

Help me to hear your still, small voice, to be soft in my heart, to be sensitive to the promptings of Your spirit. Remind me to consult You in all my doings, so that my path follows the direction best for me. In Jesus' holy name I humbly pray. Amen.

When she opened her eyes, she was alone on the verandah.

Rachel had said her piece, and had left her alone with the Lord.

And somehow, this brought tears to her eyes again. As with the news of what Gracie and Benny had done, they were tears of gratitude.

BOW K RANCH

Monday, June 20

LAST NIGHT, Tobias had driven Sylvia and the twins home in the spring wagon, and hadn't really seemed to notice when she'd encouraged the children to sit up front with him, while she perched in the back on an empty crate. Once Gracie had said her prayers and was tucked into the other twin bed, Sylvia had knelt next to her own. When she rose and slipped into the sheets, a little voice had spoken in the dark.

"Sylvia?"

"*Ja?*"

"Do you like Mark?"

Had Rachel coached her granddaughter to ask the same question? Maybe it was just as well she'd already had to answer it once today. "I like him just fine. He's a *gut* cowboy and a big help to my father."

"But do you want to marry him?"

"*Neh, Liebling.*"

A rustle of cotton sheets and quilts as the little girl turned over. "That's all right, then."

Which meant, of course, that Sylvia spent more hours lying awake than she did sleeping, and had to practically drag herself out of bed this morning in time to help Mamm make breakfast.

Mondays were wash days. When Sylvia told Gracie she'd love her help in doing the ranch's laundry, Tobias looked at her in surprise across his plate of sliced ham, egg pie, and biscuits. "She's a little young for that yet, *nix?*"

"Sylvia was helping me by her age," Mamm said serenely. "Many hands make light work, even if they're small hands."

Benny was beginning to look smug. "Guess I'll be exploring the woods by myself, then."

Tobias shook his head. "If *dei Schweschder* is getting her hands wet, it would be a *gut* day for you to learn about pumps and irrigation ditches, too," he said.

Benny clearly knew better than to refuse, but he did whine just a little. Sylvia smothered an internal glow at the way Tobias had supported her in bringing the twins' education up to date. Not the kind that involved reading and writing— though they'd get to that—but the kind that built the skills they would use all their lives.

"Everyone on the ranch has a job," Mark took it upon himself to remind Benny and Gracie through a mouthful of ham. "From cats to cows to *Kinner.*"

"We *know*," grumbled Benny. "We're ranch kids, too."

"That's right, I forgot," Mark said. "What did you do for your jobs in New Mexico?"

"I helped fold laundry," Gracie said.

"And I cleaned tack—at least, the cutting horses," Benny said. "Not the big harness for the buggy horse."

"That's a big job," Stephen said. "We could sure use some help with that around here."

Benny brightened. "Maybe I could do that today. Instead of the ditches."

Tobias gave him a nudge with his elbow. "Better to learn something new than do what you've always done—at least for now. Tack is a job for stormy days. Ditches have to be checked every day, but it's a lot nicer to learn on a sunny day like this."

"Plus, if you fall in, you dry faster," Mark joked.

Benny didn't laugh. And Sylvia realized he was not completely over his close call in the creek. "Tobias won't let him fall in," she said quietly.

The conversation turned to other things, and after breakfast, while Mamm took Gracie upstairs to collect the dirty clothes from the baskets, Tobias told Benny he'd meet him in the barn in a minute.

By some miracle, they were alone in the kitchen. Sylvia busied her hands filling the sink with hot, soapy water.

"*Denkes* to you and Kathryn for teaching Gracie how to do laundry," Tobias said at last.

"Of course. I'm sure Rachel and Susanna have showed her. This will be more of a refresher."

"Lily Anne—my late wife—she would have begun early, too. But with all the changes lately, I can't say it was uppermost in my mind."

She was pretty sure he didn't think laundry did itself. But no, she couldn't say that. Sylvia cast about for something else.

"And *denki* for what you said about the ditches," he went on, surprising her. "About Benny not falling in. I don't want him developing a fear of water after what happened."

"Maybe teach him to respect it instead," she suggested. "Gates and pumps are *gut* for that. If he's at all mechanically minded, he'll see that water is for sustaining life. While it can be dangerous in the spring, its real purpose is to be put to work, just like anything else on the ranch."

Tobias nodded thoughtfully. "*Gut* advice. It won't change its nature if he looks at it differently, but it might change how he feels toward it."

She dared a smile of agreement. His lips bent upward in return—she couldn't really call it a smile—and he went out to the mud room to put on his boots on.

After the outside door closed behind him, she washed dishes, rinsed and dried them, her hands moving automatically while she digested what had just happened. Had she and Tobias really just had a discussion about child rearing? About the work and behavior that was easy to take for granted, since the learning of them had been so long ago? She couldn't remember the first time Mamm had showed her how to work the mangle to squeeze the water out of the clothes. It was just another part of the laundry process that was so familiar she never even thought about it. She just did it, using the same agitator and mangle Mamm and Mammi and Grossmammi had used.

But laundry was a lot different from a fear of water. Walking the ditches was the best thing for Benny right now. Orderly, skinny irrigation ditches might not be very threatening, but got you just as wet if you slid into one. But since they were nowhere near as deep as the creek, even if he did fall in, he could scramble out with no harm done—to himself, at least. Getting out of a ditch without bringing down the carefully dug sides was a skill she'd learned early.

The dishes done, she shooed Mamm out of the basement to supervise Sharon and Bethany in making up the beds with fresh sheets, and she and Gracie took over. They went over to the bunkhouse and collected the hands' laundry and bedding. With Gracie ahead of her, carefully picking her way down the steps to the barn, Sylvia surreptitiously buried her nose in one of Tobias's shirts. The scent of him—cotton and wood chips and horse—was a little gift.

Laundry was a process. First the agitator, then the mangle, then hanging out to dry. She and Gracie made a game out of pegging the laundry out on the long line that extended from the back veranda over to a pine tree that was an outlier from the belt of woods that ran behind the house. The long things like sheets and pants went first, because the pine tree took them high up. Then dresses, then shirts. By the time they finished with dishtowels and underthings, the line was full and practically at eye level. Sylvia hardly had to stretch to peg them at all.

"Done!" Gracie said proudly, surveying the evidence of their hard morning's work with satisfaction. "The birds better not poop on our clean clothes."

"If they do, we can give it a scrub in the sink," Sylvia said with a grin. "We can control a lot of things, but we can't control when and where the birds poop."

Gracie wandered out into the yard, a hand over her eyes as she scanned the fields. "I wonder if Benny and Dat are done with the ditches?"

"Want to take them some coffee and cake?"

"Sure!"

Turning ditches into lessons took a lot longer than simply inspecting them every morning. The hands tended to do it before breakfast, to leave a full day for riding out or checking cattle. But when Gracie and Sylvia let themselves into the fields and closed the gate, they saw the two figures in the distance, both stooped over something. Probably a stuck water gate. Sylvia took the basket and let her companion run on ahead, jumping over the ditches as she came to them.

Sylvia heard the creak of saddle leather and turned to see Mark approaching on his horse.

"Hey," he greeted her as he rode up. "Coffee time already?"

"Maybe not, but the laundry is on the line and Gracie wanted to see her brother's progress."

"So I have a few minutes alone with you." He grinned. "What luck I just happened to be heading for the hills."

"Do you want some *Kaffee?*"

"*Neh*, I had some when I came in from the ditches on the south side. What I'd really like is another chance to take you home from singing on Sunday."

The Eicher ranch was one of the farthest away, on the outskirts of their district close under the eastern foothills. A ride home from there would take almost an hour.

"Mark—"

"Come on, Sylvia. The kids will be with Tobias, and it makes sense when we both live here, *nix?*"

Of course it did. But sometimes courtship wasn't about making sense.

She'd been anticipating this conversation. She just hadn't expected it to take place out in the middle of a field, in broad daylight.

"It does ... or it would, if I felt a different way," she said awkwardly. "But you're an employee, and I'm older than you, and ... well, I just don't feel right about it."

"Tobias is an employee, and you rode home with him last night."

"Because you were at Yoders' with the girls, and the twins —who I'm being paid to look after—had to go to bed."

"So if I'd been there at the Inn, you would have gone home with me?"

"And leave poor Sharon and Bethany to hitchhike with someone else?"

"You could have waited for us."

She was beginning to get irritated. Maybe it was the lack of sleep. "Well, I didn't. I wanted to go home, so I went with them and that's that. Hashing over the could-haves and should-haves is pointless."

"Ouch. Someone got up on the wrong side of the bed this morning."

Sylvia lost her temper in the most silent and effective way possible. She turned her back on him and strode ten yards to the ditch, jumped over it, and kept on going, the tall grasses whipping at her ankles and tapping on her skirts with the speed and length of her stride.

Mark, of course, couldn't follow. No cowboy would risk putting a cutting horse at a ditch. That was how legs got broken.

"Talk to you after supper," he called.

In a pig's eye. She didn't look back or even wave.

She was too angry. At the ripe old age of twenty-eight, she was perfectly entitled to go home when she wanted to and with whom she wanted to. An employee didn't get to make snide remarks when she did. That, she realized, was only one of the reasons she and Mark would never suit. He didn't treat her with respect. Not as his employer's daughter, not as a woman, not even as his sister in Christ. He simply expected her to do what he wanted, without consultation or talking things over or anything.

Well, if she did cool off and say yes, her only reason would be that an hour's ride home was enough time to pound into his head all the reasons she was never going to date him. And that, with any luck, would be the end of that.

GRACIE RAN UP TO BENNY AND DAT, PANTING AND OUT OF breath. "We're bringing *Kaffee*!" she announced, and peered down at Benny in the ditch. "What are you doing?"

By the time they'd walked the fourth ditch, inspected the pump, and checked all the water gates, Benny had begun to relax. Each ditch followed the same process. There was something comforting and safe in that. He looked up at his sister from his position knee deep in water, his toes squishing in the sand and weed at the bottom. His pant legs were rolled up and his boots sat on the bank.

"Inspecting this gate. See?" He shoved it. "It won't close."

"What's wrong with it?"

"A rock got in there. Dat, how are we going to get it out?"

Dat hunkered down, his hands dangling between his knees, frowning at the stubborn gate. "We tried pushing the gate, and that didn't move it. Can you get in behind it with your hands? They're smaller than mine."

Benny studied the situation gravely. Then he rolled up his shirt sleeves and bent to the task, grunting and reaching for the rock that was preventing the gate from opening in the other direction, which would guide the water down into the pasture to irrigate it. He got his fingers around the rock and with a heave, pulled it out. Water cascaded down his arm as he tossed the offender into the pasture while Dat pushed the gate into place.

"Well done, son!"

Benny beamed and warmth bloomed in his chest at Dat's

praise. Gracie hauled him out of the ditch and they both plunked down in the grass.

"Is that Mark?" Gracie squinted into the distance, where Sylvia was talking to a cowboy on horseback.

Before Benny could answer, Sylvia turned on her heel and marched toward them, jumping ditches without breaking stride, or even looking at them. Benny had never seen her cover the ground at such a pace. She was a pretty unflappable woman—maybe she and Mark had had words. What about? Not that it mattered, as long as she chased Mark away. Still, Sylvia in a temper was pretty unusual.

A minute or two later she joined them, barely breathing hard. "Here you are, taking it easy," she said with a smile. "Gracie wanted to bring you *Kaffee*. Seems it's a *gut* time."

Clearly that walk across the field had taken the edge off whatever had made her mad.

"We fixed the gate," Benny told her proudly. "A big rock fell behind it and it wouldn't close."

"Did you." Her tone held admiration. "Well done. Looks like *we* had to get wet to do it."

"It felt *gut*," he said honestly. "I was hot."

She met Dat's gaze for less than a second, but it was easy to see the quiet satisfaction in her eyes.

"Sylvia and I were talking about your helping earlier," Dat said. "I think you must be a born mechanic, like Daadi was. Making the system work takes away any fear of how deep the ditch is, or what might be swimming around in there."

Benny snorted, though he was pleased to be compared to Daadi. He knew how much Dat had loved him. "Just water skimmers and mosquito wigglers."

"Yuck." Sylvia passed Dat a piece of coffee cake, then

Benny, then Gracie. Lastly, she took one for herself and poured coffee.

The cake wasn't topped with apples today. "What are these?" Benny waggled the cake and took another bite. It was hard to identify berries sometimes after they were cooked. But he sure liked eating them.

"Blackberries, canned from last year. Some years the birds beat us to the bushes and we get hardly any, but we had a bumper crop last August. We must have canned twenty quarts, and put twenty more in freezer bags at the unit in town."

Benny was familiar with renting commercial freezer space, especially if you were a hunter going after elk or deer. Without electricity, the meat had to be stored somewhere, and Mammi always said the cost of the rental was worth it to have delicious elk stew in January, or backstrap in March.

"What did Mark want?" Gracie asked her.

"He's supposed to be fixing a fence up there." Benny waved his cake in the direction of the foothills. He'd seen the topographical map of the Keim ranch pinned to the bunkhouse wall. It stretched from the valley floor up the sides of the foothills nearly to the steep slopes of the mountains. Half Josiah's herd grazed up there, Stephen had told him, the other half was turned out on the allotment on the other side of the valley.

"Nothing much." Sylvia took a bite of cake that prevented her saying more. "He's checked the ditches on the other side. There's only three more on this side." She smiled at Benny. "Are you going to inspect them each morning with your *dat*?"

"I hope so." Benny looked up at his father for approval, and got it. "We won't be late for breakfast, will we?"

"This morning was for learning," Dat told him. "It'll go faster the more familiar they get."

"By the end of summer, you might be inspecting them on your own," Sylvia suggested.

Benny's eyes widened at such a responsibility. "All myself? But I'm only seven."

Dat couldn't help a grin. But Benny didn't see what was funny—Sylvia was a serious person, and he took what she said seriously. He was game for the job, even if it was a little intimidating.

"Inspecting doesn't take long," Dat said. "It's the pumps and gates that take the time. But if we do it together, like Pete and Danny used to, then we can save an hour at least. That will definitely get us to breakfast on time."

Benny approved this plan with a manly nod. Then he glanced at Gracie, whose eyes sparkled with the idea they'd cooked up last night after supper at Mammi's. "And maybe some night me and Gracie can camp out."

Dat coughed. Some crumbs of coffee cake must have gone down the wrong way. "Camp out where? Here in the pasture?"

Benny and Gracie rolled their eyes. "And get stepped on by cows? *Neh*, in a tent. There's tents in the tackroom, for roundup."

Even Sylvia was looking surprised. "What would you want to camp out for when the Keims have given you comfy beds?"

"Because it would be fun," Gracie said. "It was so hot yesterday. Camping would be cooler."

"That was one day, and it ended in a storm so bad Sylvia nearly went off the road," Dat reminded them. "*Neh*, I think we have enough to do without giving the Keims extra work setting up tents for you."

"Only one tent," Benny said. He had to be careful not to sound like he was arguing. That would end in an automatic no.

"I'm staying in my comfy bed," Dat went on. "Sleeping out

is just fine at roundup. It's part of the job. But not at home, where Josiah and Kathryn have made such *gut* provision for us already."

"Sylvia could sleep out with us," Gracie suggested.

A laugh erupted out of Sylvia as though something had scared it. "No, thank you. No sleeping on the hard, cold ground for me."

"We'd use the bedrolls," Benny said.

"You two." Sylvia shook her head. "Your father has already said no."

"But—" Benny began.

"Please?" Gracie begged. "Only for one night."

Dat shook his head in the way that always meant no. Really no, all kidding aside.

Benny wilted and made a rueful mouth at his sister while Sylvia started counting all the different kinds of wildflowers they could see.

But Gracie leaned close. "We'll keep trying," she whispered. "If we're out there, Dat won't be able to resist camping with us, too."

That was a fact. And once he was out there, they'd leave him alone with Sylvia, late at night, with only the stars and the crickets for company. Surely then he would see how right she was for their family.

But they had to act fast. If Mark was getting under her skin and making her mad, they might be running out of time.

$\maltese$ 12 $\maltese$

Tuesday, June 21

TUESDAYS WERE BAKING day at the Keim place, just like at the Inn, and Gracie and Benny chattered and got covered in flour and ate more chocolate chips than they folded into the batter. But Sylvia just laughed and enjoyed their antics, which weren't destructive, merely distracted. Tobias and Benny had done their morning chores and then after breakfast, Tobias had headed up into the hills on horseback with Mark to check a couple of cows whose calves were looking a little underweight. She had the twins to herself until suppertime.

She wondered where their odd desire to camp out had come from. Some of the other *Kinner* at church? Or were they just being seven, when camping seemed unusual and brave, like when their father camped out on the mountain during roundup and regaled them with the adventure of it when he got back. At least, her father had always done that. Sylvia had been the last in the family to be allowed to go. She'd been nine, her legs finally long enough to reach the stirrups of a cutting horse. Then, camping in the tents in the alpine meadows had been exciting, and Dat frying bacon and making coffee over a fire so unusual it gave the food a whole new flavor.

But as the years passed, Sylvia had been just as happy to stay home and help her mother and the other women prepare the big roundup meal. It was a way to say thank you to their friends and neighbors for helping to bring the cattle down from the mountains. The Amish in the valley helped each other out for big jobs like that. Roundup meant almost a whole year's income for a cattle rancher, and since no one outfit could do it alone, everyone pitched in.

But today was the first day of summer, according to the calendar tacked on the wall by the door, and after spring turnout, the ranch had settled into the routine of summer work. Sylvia saw that the twins already knew how to make chocolate chip cookies (it helped when you could read the recipe, Gracie informed her). While Sharon and Bethany beat cake batter, she and the children took out several trays of cookies in shifts, then turned the propane oven over to the girls.

Mamm came in, a duster in one hand. "Oh good, you're almost done. Sylvia, I forgot to tell you that Willard Zook mentioned on Sunday that he'd like you to come by. They're working on producing their own honey, and they wanted your opinion on the flavor."

Sylvia stared at her, while Benny snuck a cookie off the cooling rack and bit into it blissfully. "*My* opinion?"

Her mother nodded. "Evidently he heard you last week at the fellowship meal. Something about bees and garlic?"

"I was talking with Patricia King about *chickens* eating garlic. And how you can taste it in their eggs."

"Ew," said Gracie, swiping a cookie off the rack herself.

Her mother shrugged. "The same principles might apply to bees, though I have to say I've never noticed it myself. Anyhow, he wanted you to do a taste test. Says some people are more sensitive to flavors than others, and you might be one of them."

Sylvia resigned herself. Dat and the Zook brothers were *gut* friends, and goodness knew the latter would do anything to help if a person needed it. She would just have to put on a smile and do this little thing for Willard without complaint ... or any suspicion that Mamm hadn't given up hope where he was concerned.

"Looks like we're going out this afternoon," she told the twins with a smile. "Maybe we can drop in on Mammi and Susanna afterward."

So, after the lunch dishes were done, and Mamm had packed a plastic tub full of cookies for Willard and Zeke, the children helped her hitch Rhoda to the buggy. The buggy showed no signs of its adventure in the mud of Creekside Lane, having been washed down once they got home. Luckily the fields and roads had dried up since that eventful Sunday.

"Even the flowers have perked up again," Gracie observed as they clip-clopped down the Keim lane to the road. "They were pretty flat after that storm."

"So was I," Sylvia confessed. "I'm glad the sun is out again. And I bet you are, too, Rhoda."

The horse swiveled her ears at the sound of her name, and jogged on. The four miles over to the Zook place seemed to go by in just a few minutes. The twins, naturally, headed for the barn and the meadow to say hello to the goats, while Sylvia knocked on the farmhouse's back door and walked in.

"That didn't take long." Willard looked up with a smile

from a row of canning jars on the counter filled with golden liquid. "Are those for us?"

"Baked this morning, with the help of Benny and Gracie."

"It's *gut* you're teaching the boy to do things in the kitchen. Makes him less likely to starve before he finds himself a *Fraa*."

Sylvia snorted. "Let's not get ahead of ourselves. He's only seven. But Mamm feels that even a boy ought to know his way around a stove and what to do with the pots and pans. If he takes up ranching, there's many a bunkhouse where the hands have to do their own cooking."

"I've heard tell of one or two who couldn't do much more than open a can of beans and set it on the flame," Willard said, leaning on the counter and sampling a cookie. "Hands don't tend to gain weight while they're working, but an employer doesn't want them so skinny they lose their strength, either."

"True." The Zook brothers were unusual in a couple of ways. One, they were in their early fifties and still unmarried. They'd long ago decided the dignity of age deserved a beard. Neither of them were clean-shaven, like single men such as Mark or Stephen. And two, both of them had a talent for the kitchen and dairy. Their cheeses were shipped all over Montana and even beyond, and all the restaurants and groceries in Mountain Home carried them. Even the *Englisch* ones.

"Mamm tells me you need a guinea pig," she went on when he didn't seem inclined to talk. "Is that your honey there?"

"I thought you might be a better taster than *mei Bruder*. He thinks anything sweet is *gut*. But if I'm going to sell this honey over to Yoder's Variety Store or even the *Englisch* supermarket, it's got to be a little bit special, like the bees who made it."

She walked over to admire the half-dozen jars lined up in the sunlight. "Where are your hives?"

"At the moment they're on Noah King's land, but with the work starting there, we'll have to tell the bees they're moving. I had a word with young Sara Miller at the hay farm. She and Joshua have a lot of wild roses and other flowers along their fences. They've got a couple fields planted in alfalfa. And she's planted a herb garden for her cures. I think the bees would like it there."

"I think they would, too." He spoke of the insects as though they were people, the way Gracie talked about their chickens. It wasn't very Amish, but there was a kind of charm in it. And goodness knew the Zook brothers had a way with living things. "Well, if you're ready for me to taste it, I should. I don't want to leave the twins alone with the goats too long."

"It's all right. Zeke is out there."

He got a long spoon from a drawer, the kind people ate ice cream sodas with at the shop in town. He dipped it in one of the jars and offered it to her, one hand under the spoon to catch the drips.

She took it, tasted half the spoonful, let the flavor fill her mouth, then finished the rest. She couldn't resist licking the spoon clean. "Willard, it's wonderful."

"Tell me what you taste."

The flavor still lingered. "I almost wonder if the bees have been spending all their time at the hay farm anyway. It tastes the way a meadow full of wildflowers smells."

"Or alfalfa?"

She smiled. "Maybe, now that you mention it. What do you think?"

"I've kept bees on and off over the years, but no one flavor ever stood out. Lots of apple blossom and wild flowers for them, but nothing that would predominate. Until the farms hereabouts started putting in alfalfa for the cattle ranches. It makes a sweeter honey, I think. And you find a scent?"

"No," she said thoughtfully. "More like an aftertaste in the mouth. Sweet, yes, but this lovely finish to it. Mind you, hungry *Kinner* and hands would probably never notice it. But with just one spoonful, I did."

"Now see, I didn't. I don't taste garlic in eggs, either. Mind you, not too much of that growing around here."

"Well, I'm glad I could help. Now I'd best collect the twins. Their grandmother will be glad to see them."

"Sylvia, just a moment."

It had been several years since Willard Zook had called her by her name. *Maedscher*, maybe, when she was small. But in all the time they'd lived in the same district, eaten meals together, gone on roundup together, he and his brother had conversed with her parents, and the hands, or her sisters' husbands. Not so often with her.

He wiped off the jar of honey she'd tasted, screwed on the lid, and handed it to her.

"*Denki*, Willard," she said. "But if you can sell this, you should."

He shook his head. "You did me a service. Consider it payment."

"A spoonful of honey isn't exactly a service. More like a treat."

"But with what you said, I can tell the young man who makes labels for us what to put on it. It's a new product, so I wanted to get it right. And while you're here, maybe I ought to introduce you to the bees."

Her brows rose. "Introduce me?" To insects? Maybe the Zook brothers were even odder than people thought.

"*Ja. Kumm mit.*"

Mystified, she went out into the meadow with him, following him through the grass past the stakes and yellow string. The bee boxes sat close under the eaves of the trees that ran next to the creek, and bees glimmered in the sunshine as they zoomed in and out of their homes.

They stopped about ten feet away. "Bees," he said to them, "I hope you are well, and I thank you for the honey you gave us this week."

The bees did not reply, but they didn't fly away in fear, either, or start looking for somewhere to land and sting.

"This here is Sylvia. She enjoyed your honey, too." He glanced at her from under one graying, bushy eyebrow. "Thank them."

What did one say to bees? "Thank you, bees. You turned the alfalfa into something wonderful, and I appreciate it."

Maybe it was her imagination, but now she could hear their humming, as though they were acknowledging her thanks. She half expected one or two to land on her and sting her, but they merely went about their business. She glanced at Willard, wondering if there was more to an insect introduction.

"They accept you," he said.

"Until I try to squash one, I expect."

"You wouldn't do that. You're the kind to take a spider outside rather than squash it."

She had to laugh. He must have seen her do it after church.

"Besides, honeybees don't sting unless they're provoked." He swallowed. "I wonder, Sylvia..."

There was her name again. Did he have other jars of honey he wanted her to taste? "*Ja?*"

"I wonder how you feel about courting."

Courting.

Courting?

He must be making a joke. Though he didn't look very amused. "I'm in favor of it in general," she said with a laugh.

"I meant in specific. How you feel about you and me courting."

Willard Zook courting her? Holy smokes, he was almost as old as her father! What was in the air this summer? First Mark, now Willard?

"I—well, I—"

"If you were inclined, I'd make sure Zeke had his supper and was out in the barn when you came over. I'm well off. The dairy business is doing well, and our parents paid off the farm long ago."

"Willard ... goodness me, I never ... I mean, I don't look at you that way."

"I didn't look at you that way, either, until I was talking with your Mamm at spring Communion. She'd like to see you married, and the more I thought about it, the more I thought I might, too."

Her mouth opened and closed at the magnitude of Mamm's betrayal. Spring Communion had been a month ago, and not a word had she said, other than pushing her at random men every now and again. But there was the errand to fetch the cheese. And now this honey-tasting business, which clearly Mamm had arranged with Willard beforehand. Probably on Sunday.

How could she? When Sylvia had told her specifically to cease and desist?

Willard nodded, as though she had spoken. "I know it's a surprise. But no need to give an answer right away. You think it over. Take as much time as you like. I'll need plenty of time myself, to bring Zeke around to the idea."

Zeke! So the general feeling among the women in the valley

had its roots in truth. Marriage to one of the Zook brothers wouldn't mean two husbands, of course, as she'd heard Sharon and Bethany giggling about more than once, but it would certainly mean a household of three.

And what about children ...?

But here Sylvia's imagination failed her. It was pointless even to consider it. Even before that kiss with Tobias, she'd known no other man would do for her but him. Even if he never saw her in that way, even if both of them stayed single the rest of their lives, her heart would always belong to him.

She would not lead this good man on by pretending to think it over, when there was no hope.

"*Denki*, Willard, for thinking so well of me," she said slowly. "I'm honored by it. But I have to tell you ... there's someone else."

Willard took a long breath and let it out again. "Tobias Miller."

The shock rang through her as though she'd been struck like a bell. "How on earth?"

He lifted one shoulder. "You're caring for his *Kinner*. And I've seen your face when you look at him. Not often. But often enough."

"I—I'm sorry." He was the second person to tell her that her face had given her away. Apparently the only person who hadn't noticed was Tobias himself.

"Don't be. I thought I would take my chances. *Denki* for letting me say my piece."

His head was bowed and something close to affection made her take his rough, callused hand in both of hers. "You're a good man, Willard Zook. Any woman would be glad to have a place at your side. Any woman whose heart wasn't already filled with—" She may as well say it. "With hopeless feelings for someone else that aren't returned."

He met her gaze as he squeezed her hand, then released it. "I wouldn't give up all hope. *Der Herr* works in strange ways. And a woman who is already acting as a mother only needs a hop and a skip to actually be one."

She smiled at this picture. "From your lips to *Gott*'s ears."

"I want you to be happy, Sylvia. If I can't have a try at making you so, then I pray that he'll have the sense to do it. And now, here come your little charges," he said, his tone changing as the high voices of the twins hailed them from across the field. "You need anything from us, you have only to ask."

"Denki, mei Freind," she said.

And as the twins joined them, full of facts about goats clearly gleaned from Zeke, he took a little hand in each of his to walk over and introduce them to the bees, too.

Sylvia may have declined a suitor, she reflected as she watched their awestruck faces, but God had given her a blessing and allowed her to keep a friend.

❧ 13 ☙

AFTER A VISIT at the Inn with Rachel and Susanna, where Sylvia felt as though she had more to conceal than to share, she and the twins went home with one or two extra shirts for Benny and another dress and *Kapp* for Gracie. She watched for an opportunity to talk with Mamm all afternoon and during the evening, but her mother must have sensed it, because she was always busy or there were people around.

Sylvia resigned herself to going over a handful of spelling words with Benny, much to his disgust, but Tobias backed her up.

"You already knew you'd have to work on your spelling words while you were here," he told his son quietly. "No point putting up a fuss now."

He read the paper in the porch swing while she and the children sat on the steps of the wraparound porch with paper and pencils in the warm evening light. He didn't watch them, but his presence made Benny a lot less likely to whine and wriggle. Instead, he seemed to accept his fate and applied himself to his paper as well as a child could be expected to on a summer evening.

It was dusk when the children were done, and Tobias took Benny off to the bunkhouse and bed, while she gathered up pencils and paper and took them upstairs with Gracie. When Sylvia came back down to an empty kitchen, she peeked out the screen door. Mamm had relaxed her guard and sat in the porch swing. She seized her moment.

Seating herself next to her, Sylvia pushed the swing with one foot and tried not to smile when Mamm pretended to enjoy the view of yard and barn instead of looking at her.

"Mamm, we need to talk."

"We talk all day long, *Liewi*."

"Not about Willard Zook, we don't. Or Mark Steiner, either."

Mamm's cheeks colored. "Two *gut* men who deserve a *gut* woman."

"Maybe so, but they don't deserve a matchmaker. You've got to stop, Mamm. I had to wound that *gut* man's feelings today, and I didn't like how it made me feel. Not one bit."

"You wounded his feelings?"

"Well, I couldn't very well string him along and let him hope when there isn't any."

Mamm turned to face her in the swing, her eyes wide. "Are you telling me that Willard Zook proposed to you? And you turned him down?"

"I wouldn't say *proposed*. He asked if he could court me. And *ja*, I turned him down."

"But why?" Mamm's eyes held dismay, her tone a complete lack of understanding.

There were so many reasons why that Sylvia could only give

the most obvious one, not the one that really mattered. "For heaven's sake, Mamm, he's Dat's age!"

"Nothing wrong with that."

"And I suppose you think the Zooks are a bargain, like soap. Buy one, get one free."

"Sylvia, that's unkind."

"It's what every single woman in the valley thinks."

"Then they need an attitude adjustment. Dozens of families have relatives living with them. It's our way."

"Well, I'm not going to be one of them. Not that way. And while we're on the subject, I need you to stop throwing Mark Steiner at me, too." She put up a hand as her mother took a breath to protest that she was doing no such thing. "Mamm, I'm serious. I don't look at Mark like that."

"He certainly seems to look at *you* like that."

"Then I'm sorry to disappoint him. But he and I are incompatible."

"And you know this how?"

"He doesn't respect me, for one thing."

Now she'd shocked her mother. "How can you say that? He's always offering you the best part of the roast at dinner, or passing you another helping of dessert. And he makes an effort to sit opposite you at the fellowship meal after church so he can talk to you. Get acquainted as more than the boss's daughter. I've never seen him do anything that wasn't respectful."

"He won't let me finish a sentence, for one."

Mamm gazed at her, *Is that all?* written on her face.

"It's a little thing, but it matters. It tells me he doesn't think what I have to say is important."

"You think what you have to say is important? *Pass the butter* is important?"

"Now you're just distracting."

"I'm cautioning you against pride, *Dochder*. A woman's voice is never more important than a man's, just like a man's voice is never more important than God's."

"I'll try to remember that the next time a man leaps out of a slewing buggy on the edge of a slope and lets the horse run away without a driver."

Mamm was finally silenced. After a minute, she said, "He was trying to get to the halter, to control Rhoda's head."

"I don't doubt he was. But that wasn't how it felt when I had to grab the reins from all the way in the back and try to get myself on to the front seat, all while keeping the buggy from going over the edge."

"I wish they would pave that road."

"So do I." But would that solve Mark's poor judgement? He was normally so good with animals, and a hard worker. But a woman had to live with the whole man, not just the part that the world around them saw.

She remembered Tobias, doing so calmly what Mark had meant to do in stopping the panicked horse. How his presence on the porch silently supported her when Benny balked at his spelling words. In ways great and small, he showed her he valued her.

But even when she'd lost her head and kissed him, he hadn't shown any more than that. He valued her as a sister in Christ. What would it take for him to value her as a woman? As a wife?

Mamm gave a sigh. "I only want you to be happy, *Liewi*."

Sylvia took her mother's hand, work-worn and strong. "I know, Mamm. But do you think you could leave my matrimonial prospects in *Gott*'s hands? I have faith that He'll direct me to the one He wants for me. I mean, look at the Millers on the Circle M over this past year."

"He's done a mighty work there, I must say." Mamm huffed a laugh. "I hope He'll turn His eyes toward you once He gets done with them. Though if Susanna and Stephen are any indication, He isn't finished with that family yet."

Sylvia laughed, too, though she felt like sighing. "Is that what that *Englisch* hymn means? *Wait on the Lord?*"

At last, they shared a giggle that held no undercurrents, just the surprise of humor. Sylvia leaned over and gave her mother a kiss on the cheek. "I should go check on Gracie, and go to bed myself."

Mamm nodded. She touched Sylvia's hand as she rose. "You know I meant it, don't you? I only want God's blessings for you."

"*Ja*, Mamm. I know."

She went quietly into the house. Who knew whether Mamm would take her words to heart. But at least Sylvia had said what she needed to say.

Now she could only hope that her treacherous face didn't give her mother any ideas. She could imagine no humiliation worse than Mamm trying to matchmake her with Tobias when he'd already made it very plain where his heart would always belong.

Worse even than the little matchmakers who had already tried so hard and failed in their attempts.

Thursday, June 23

"Please can we go to town, too, and have ice cream?"

If there was anything Tobias found difficult to resist, it was Gracie's big blue eyes. They were so like Lily Anne's that it gave him a pang to the heart every time. Which meant that saying no became almost impossible.

The hydraulic pump Josiah had ordered to replace the one that had been giving him and Benny trouble for days had come in at the feed store, and needed to be picked up. He'd made the mistake of saying so within earshot of his *Kinner*, who had jumped on their opportunity like a hen on a grasshopper.

"Pleeeeease?"

"I don't think so, Gracie. It's a business errand, there and back, if Benny and I want to get that pump replaced out there in the field before supper."

Benny's face went from being happy that his father was including him in a cowboy's work to aghast that said work would deprive him of the coveted treat.

"But Dat, what about Sylvia's errands?"

"What about them?" He could hear her in the kitchen with Sharon and Bethany, finishing up the lunch dishes. His, Stephen's, and Mark's chores today had kept them fairly near the home paddocks, so they'd come to the house for lunch instead of packing it as usual.

"She's going to teach me to make a quilt," Gracie said, her eyes sparkling. "And how to use the treadle machine. She has fabric here, but I get to choose some for my very own, too."

First the washer and the mangle, now the sewing machine? Tobias felt a rush of gratitude to Sylvia for stepping into a mother's place so quietly yet efficiently. Susanna and Mamm would have got around to teaching Gracie themselves, he was pretty sure, but snowy winter days were a ways off yet, and if he was keeping Benny busy in the early mornings, it was good of Sylvia to give Gracie's mind as much to occupy it as her brother's had.

He was also well aware that with these two, you had to strike while the iron was hot. If he waited until next week, Gracie might have found something else to interest her, and it might involve a lot more mischief than learning to sew. He didn't want to test Sylvia's patience and make her decide she didn't want to be a nanny anymore.

"All right. If we run out of time, I suppose you and I can install the pump in the morning. We'll just have to hope that rusty old pump lasts the night."

Cheering, the twins ran to tell Sylvia that she could come with them. The ice cream parlor wasn't exactly on the agenda, but even Lily Anne would have understood.

"You can stop to smell the roses as well as dig and fertilize them, Tobias," she'd tease him. And he'd say, "But without the digging and fertilizing, you'd have no blossoms to smell." And then she'd kiss him and say how nice it was that they agreed, and change the subject. Like maybe he should buy tamales from Hortensia, one of the Four Winds hands' wives, to give his own wife a holiday from cooking.

He hadn't had a tamale since they'd left New Mexico.

Fifteen minutes later, the buggy hitched up, he was at the reins with Sylvia in the passenger seat and the twins in the back, practically bouncing with excitement. Since the tourist traffic in Mountain Home was on the rise now that school was out, he tied the horse to the rail in the buggy shed at Stolzfus Smith & Farrier, which was next to Yoder's Variety Store and across Main Street from Rose Garden Quilts. There was no street parking to be had, and he'd just as soon Rhoda was out of reach of curious hands anyway.

The ice cream shop was four doors down from the quilt shop, and only open from Memorial Day to Labor Day. What were the odds his progeny would forget about that part of the outing?

He and Benny went to fetch the pump while the girls went to see Rose. They took their time, but evidently quilt shops were fascinating places, because they still weren't back when he and Benny had finished securing the pump in the rear of the buggy.

"Come on," he said, taking his son's hand for the dash across the highway. "We'd better roust them out of there before Sylvia has to take all that fabric out of my wages."

The shop was a welcoming place, with one of Malena Miller's pieces hanging in the window and several more by other valley quilters on the walls. The counter was polished pine, the racks of fabric made of the same, giving it a lightness that had less to do with the skylights above than the warmth of wood.

A pair of young Amish women were inside, their heads together with those of Sylvia and Gracie as the serious business of choosing fabrics was conducted. Rose Stolzfus waved them over. "Tobias, do you know Noah King's sisters? Clara and Patricia King."

"You came to the barn raising last week." He shook hands, and looked down at Gracie, who carried a bolt nearly as tall as she was. "What have you got there, *Dochder*?"

"I want this one too."

With a laugh, Patricia King, the taller of the girls, hefted it up on the cutting table with a couple of others. "She has a *gut* eye for color, your young quilter."

"Sylvia is teaching me," Gracie said.

"I started at about your age," Patricia said. "Have you thought about thread?" Gracie looked from her to Sylvia to Rose. Patricia passed a hand over the top bolt. "Thread is important. Since we Amish don't use patterned fabrics for our own quilts, we think about what color our quilting thread will be. Sometimes it's different from the piecing thread, because it's invisible in the seams."

"Oh." Gracie looked at the short stack of bolts. "But I have blue and green and raspberry. What color goes with all of those?"

Patricia sorted the stack from light to dark. "I'd use a dark blue thread to sew with, and with the nature colors you've chosen, maybe you'd think about what patterns you'd quilt. Feathers might be nice in blue thread. Or leaves in green, *nix?*"

"We're going to keep it simple," Sylvia said, since Gracie was beginning to sink under the weight of all these decisions.

Tobias wisely kept his mouth shut. His contributing to this discussion would be like his daughter advising what grease would be best in the pump.

"A pink and green nine-patch set on point in a blue and black field," Sylvia mused.

"*Gut*, simple design choices," Patricia said, nodding. "So all we have to think of for the quilting thread would be which fabric you'd see the most of."

"Blue," Gracie said promptly. "I like blue."

"So do I." Patricia smiled at her, dimples flashing. "*Kumm mit*, and I'll show you. Rose must have twenty shades of blue thread. Better bring that bolt."

At long last the decisions were made, the fabric cut, the thread chosen. As she wrapped Gracie's purchases, Rose lifted an eyebrow at Patricia.

"You've been a great help," she said. "Have you ever thought of working in a fabric shop?"

The girl's surprise made a flush come into her cheeks. "Well ... *neh*. I'm pretty sure I'm better at buying it than selling it to someone."

"I could use some help in here now that the summer tourists are coming. You seem to have a talent for color and helping people make decisions without telling them what to do. That's more rare than you might think."

"I—well—my goodness—"

Clara poked her sister to stop her stammering.

"Talk it over with your family," Rose said easily. "It's only minimum wage, but I could give you as many hours as you wanted, especially after four o'clock. We open at ten and close at eight."

"*Denki*, Rose," Patricia said breathlessly. "I'll let you know."

Tobias and his *Kinner* followed them out, with Sylvia bringing up the rear.

"I like Patricia," Gracie announced, her arms filled with the bag of cut fabric. "Can we have ice cream now?"

So much for hoping they would forget. Tobias reminded himself there was no sin in smelling the roses. "I'll put your things in the buggy and meet you in the shop."

When he got there, he found them still at the counter, where more important decisions required careful consideration. But a line was forming behind them.

"Hurry up, you two. We don't want to keep these folks waiting."

They gave their orders, and Sylvia asked for a cup with a scoop each of salted caramel and cheesecake. Tobias usually just ate whatever was dishing up at supper. He was not used to so many choices. The chalkboard of flavors on the wall all ran together, and he could practically feel the impatience of the people in the line.

"I'll have the same," he blurted.

They paid and took their ice creams out to a pair of tables on the sidewalk, where a lone *Englisch* man sat at the other one. He was in his late fifties, skinny and lanky like many of the ranchers in the area. But he didn't have the look of a rancher. There was something sad about his eyes, though his cup of ice cream was empty, which told Tobias he'd enjoyed it.

"Hello," the man said as the children dug in and Tobias cautiously tasted his ice cream. Salted caramel turned out not to be disgusting, but delicious.

"Hallo," Benny said. "You're staying at the Inn, aren't you? You've been here for ages. Haven't you caught any fish?"

"Benny," Sylvia said, her cheeks reddening.

"It's all right." The man nodded to them. "You're Tobias, right? Rachel's oldest?" Tobias introduced Sylvia and the children. "My name is Howard Layton. You're right, Benny. I've been here a week or two. But I can't go home quite yet."

"Why not?" Benny was making quick work of his double scoop grasshopper ice cream, as though he wanted to get to the waffle cone without wasting time.

"Because I've lost something, and I can't go home until I find it."

"A sheep?" They'd been reading about the shepherd and his ninety-nine sheep. "A coin?"

"Close. A ring."

His children exchanged a glance and Tobias saw it. Now, what did that mean?

"What kind of a ring?" Gracie asked, just a little too casually.

Sylvia was gazing at Gracie from under her lashes, as if she'd heard that note in her voice, too. She had long lashes. Dark. Dark eyebrows, too, in contrast with her blond hair.

He blinked himself back to the matter at hand as Howard said, "A gold wedding ring. Mine, as it happens. I lost it in the creek below the Inn the second day I was here, and I've been fishing for it more than for trout ever since."

Benny looked down at his ice cream cone. A rivulet of

green mint was about to cascade over his thumb, but he made no move to lick it off.

"Can't you get another one?" Gracie asked him, neatly cleaning up her own blueberry and lemon rivulets, not letting a single drop of goodness escape.

"Wedding rings don't work that way," Howard told her gently. "My wife put it on my finger when we were married twenty-five years ago, and it hasn't left my hand since. I think maybe the cold water in the creek made my fingers shrink. I didn't even notice it was gone until I waded out to put my gear away."

Benny roused himself and caught the green rivulet just in time. "Will you get in trouble from your wife if you go home without it?"

Howard's face turned bleak. "She died the winter before last, at our home in Texas. She was lighting candles one night when the power went out. She had a stroke, and when she fell, she knocked over a bunch of burning candles. By the time the firefighters got there, the whole house had gone up."

"I'm so sorry," Sylvia whispered in horror. "You lost your wife and your home, too?"

He rubbed a pale ring of skin on the fourth finger of his left hand. "It's the only thing I have of her. That, and a couple of her oil paintings she gave to the kids. I live with my son in Phoenix now. He came here with me the first week, but he had to go back to work, and I stayed on. To find the ring."

Benny handed his ice cream cone to Tobias, who took the sticky thing automatically, his mind still filled with this poor man's tragedy.

His son dug in his pocket and pulled something out. "Is this it?"

Howard's face turned red, then pale at the sight of the plain gold band. "Is there an inscription?"

"What's that?"

"Writing. On the inside."

"I can't read it. We don't learn cursive until next year."

"May I?"

Benny's hesitation was more like a tensing and releasing of the muscles in his hand, but he handed it over. Howard looked at the inside of the ring, and silently, slowly, a tear welled up and rolled down his sunburned cheek. *"Love never fails,"* he said hoarsely. "You found it, you blessed boy."

Now it was Benny's turn to blush as his earnest gaze met that of Tobias. "I wasn't going to keep it, Dat," he said, as though Tobias had spoken.

"I know," he said softly. "You kept it safe just long enough to make a man happy instead. That kind of happiness is a rare thing."

Silently, Sylvia pulled one of her embroidered handkerchiefs from her apron pocket and gave it to Howard, who was openly weeping now as he slid his wedding ring into place.

"How can I ever thank you?"

Benny was giving this serious consideration, so Tobias stepped in hastily. "You already have. I'm glad my son was able to help. But now we have to be on our way."

They left him smiling through his tears as he ambled up Main Street in the direction of the Inn, still clutching the damp handkerchief. Tobias had a feeling he'd be heading home to Arizona soon. It was *gut* he had family to go to. Heaven knew he'd learned to value his own family after Lily Anne died. His brothers had ridden at his side, unwilling to leave him alone out on the range. Susanna had made all his favorite things to eat for months, even when food tasted like straw and he had to eat it or he wouldn't have the strength to work. And the twins ... well, they gave him two irrepressible reasons to live.

Even in the darkest moments, when he'd been unwilling to face the reality of Lily Anne's death, the thought of his children—to think of, to work for—could pull him out of despair. They were the best of her. Gracie's compassion and need for order. Benny's curiosity and sense of adventure. All facets of Lily Anne's personality, yet blended with his own to create individuals who were unique and yet endearingly familiar.

Howard Layton's life had held both love and tragedy, like that of Tobias. He was carrying on, like Tobias.

But Tobias was not walking up the street alone. Benny had taken his hand to cross Main Street, and hadn't let it go. Sylvia walked just ahead, laughing with Gracie over goodness knew what. And *der Herr* looked down upon them all on this beautiful summer day, making His presence felt in the warmth of the sunshine and the privilege of doing something for a stranger.

Suddenly Tobias was flooded with gratitude.

As though she felt a change in the wind, Sylvia looked over her shoulder and smiled, the organdy strings of her *Kapp* lifting in the breeze.

What a beautiful smile she had.

It was only later, when they were back at the Bow K and he was unhitching Rhoda, that he realized her smile had stayed with him. And for the first time, he appreciated it for what it was, and didn't feel the need to compare it to Lily Anne's.

❧ 14 ❧

THAT EVENING WAS SO soft and warm that Sylvia felt the old teenage restlessness come upon her again. In those days, a west wind and the scent of the wild roses used to fill her heart with longing—for what, she didn't know then. A boyfriend. A life like her eldest sister had, in the softer climate where she and her husband lived. It was only as time went on that Sylvia got to know herself better, and when the west wind blew and that longing came over her, she had learned to recognize it.

A yearning to belong.

Oh, she belonged here at home, on the ranch. But the time for that kind of belonging had worn a little thin; it ought to be coming to an end. She belonged, as Mamm was all too fond of telling her, in her own home with her own husband and family.

Well, it wasn't as if she hadn't tried. Or that a man or two hadn't.

Was she being too fussy? Asking for too much? When *Gott* presented two perfectly *gut* candidates to her in the same month, was it really her place to say no and stubbornly hold out for the one she couldn't have?

Maybe that was a question for Mamm. Or for the bishop. Though her nerve failed her at saying such things out loud to either of them.

She had walked out past the house to the belt of pines and fir that acted both as a windbreak and as a kind of dividing line between the home place and the first of the two grazing fields that stretched for a mile before the ground began to rise into the foothills. As that teenage girl, it had been the only place she could find privacy for both dreams and tears.

Lots of tears, especially as the young women in her buddy bunch married and moved away, their friendship maintained by circle letters, but their presence and companionship only a memory. Their letters held news of children and home renovations and even travel. Hers were thin in comparison, though she'd become pretty good at making even the same old a little more interesting with humor and observation.

Well, she wouldn't be telling them about Willard anytime soon. He didn't deserve to be giggled over, and she was all too afraid that one or two of her correspondents would read her a lecture about being too choosy.

A stick snapped on the trail behind her and she turned, half expecting an escaped cow. Or worse, Mark Steiner.

"It's only me," Tobias said, clearly surprised to have seen her white *Kapp* glimmering ahead of him in the dusk. "Sylvia? What are you doing out here? I thought the family had all gone to bed."

She breathed deeply to quiet her galloping heart. A cow was a danger a whole lot less threatening than a beautiful evening with Tobias in it.

"I walk out here when I need some thinking time," she said.

"Oh ... sorry. I can go. Do you mind company?"

"*Neh*. I'd much rather have you than—" *Mark*. "—the runaway cow I thought was behind me."

He chuckled, and she waved at the black shape of a fallen log just where the trail crested and dropped away into a dry creek bed and the grasslands began. "I usually stop here." She seated herself on its wide bulk, its rough bark worn smooth, probably by the behinds of several generations of Keims.

He joined her, respectfully giving her the last thing she wanted: ample room. "Nice night."

"I was just thinking about when I was a teenager and used to come out here. There was something about the west wind that made me wish I could jump off this little bluff and fly."

"The desire for freedom?"

She lifted a shoulder. "It was different every time. Mostly my head was full of one boy or another."

With a sound of agreement in his throat, he said, "Pretty common at that age. I used to worry I'd never find a girl to make a home with. In the Ventana Valley, where I grew up, the church started to dwindle right about the time I was taking an interest in the subject. One by one the families moved away. In the end, there was only us and the bishop's family left."

Now, there was a sobering thought. "That must have been hard for your brothers. It's one thing to have a choice, even if you choose not to make it. It's completely different to have no choice at all."

"I was lucky. Lily Anne's family did move away, but not until after we were married. But you're right—Gideon and Seth didn't complain too much about moving here. They haven't had much time for courting, though. Onkel Reuben keeps them busy on the Circle M."

"Summer on a ranch." She nodded, though he probably couldn't see. The stars were pricking out in the deep bowl of the sky. "Autumn will be on us soon enough, and they'll have plenty of long evenings for that."

"I guess that means you'll have to wait until the snow flies for Mark, too."

Shocked, she couldn't decide whether or not his light-hearted tone meant he was fishing, or if under it he was serious.

"Mark will have to wait longer than that," she finally said. "He's asked me again if I'd like a ride home with him on Sunday. Last week the twins gave me a *gut* reason not to go to the singing. But I won't have them on a church Sunday unless..." She waited.

"Are you asking me to lend you my children to protect you from Mark?" He laughed. "I didn't think he was that bad. I got the impression Kathryn was all in favor."

"She's all in favor of anyone who will take me off her hands." The moment the bitter words were out, she regretted them. "I didn't mean that. Mamm only wants to see me happy. That's all that matters to her. I just wish she wasn't so obvious about bringing people to my attention."

"At least she doesn't mind if they're ranchers. Lily Anne's mother didn't want us to get married. She'd learned all too well how hard the ranch life is. But she was from Holmes County. She hadn't grown up with it. She never really understood how much Lily Anne loved the Ventana country. All she wanted was to raise a family and for the children to love it, too. And then—"

His throat closed and he was silent.

Sylvia sat in the windy darkness, unable to say a word.

After a moment, he said, "So, are you going to go?"

She didn't misunderstand what he meant. "I haven't decided. But I suppose I'll have to, soon."

"A ride home with a man does mean more than just a convenience if both of you live in the same place," he allowed. "Not interested in courting?"

"Not with him," she said bluntly. "Unfortunately, both my parents have a little notion about us getting married and Mark taking over the ranch when the time comes."

"Mark." She'd surprised him with the long view. "Not one of your older brothers?"

"They have their own places—one near St Ignatius and the other down in Rosebud County. Of all of us, it's been me who wanted to stay here in the valley. Everyone else was looking to what lay beyond these mountains, but I never did. I liked what was inside them best. I feel safe here. Despite the blizzards and the cold and never being able to grow peaches, it's my home."

"It does have a way of growing on you." He crossed his boots at the ankle and leaned back on his hands. "What do *you* think about Mark running the ranch?"

She shook her head. "Since its long-term success doesn't depend on his marrying me, the Bow K is probably safe from him." He shifted a little. "Oh, I don't mean he's a bad rancher. He's probably the opposite. He'd do all right, though if my parents ever sold up, it would be Stephen and Susanna I'd rather see on the place. Stephen just ... understands it. To Mark, it's a job he happens to be good at. He'd probably be good at buggy-making, too, but he doesn't have to marry anyone to have a permanent job in that line of work."

"Stephen and Susanna could never afford to buy this place."

"My father will never sell it. It has to go to family, and they'd build a *Daadi Haus* and he would herd cows until he fell out of the saddle."

Tobias chuckled. "That sounds like Josiah."

She didn't know whether to ask or not, but since they were being so honest ... "Is that what you wanted with Lily Anne? To run the ranch after Rachel handed over the reins?"

"For sure and certain. Stephen only became foreman after my father and Lily Anne both died ... because for a while there, I just couldn't see how I was going to go on. But I did. I needed work. To not think about—" He stopped. Cleared his throat. "Funny how work and *Kinner* both have a way of saving you."

I wouldn't know. But she could imagine it.

"The love for the land still lay under the ruins of the other things I loved," he finally said. "I was working my way into it when everything changed. And here we are."

"I love the land, too," she mused. "We think of it as unchanging, but really, in less time than you think, it can all be different. That neurological center over east of town wasn't there when I was a girl. But it's saved many a life, even if cattle don't graze on that parcel anymore."

"I wish something could have saved—" In the light of the rising moon, the bleached straw of his hat moved up and down, the brim leaving all but his mouth and chin in shadow. "It was my fault," he whispered.

The breeze tickled the back of her neck and she shivered. "How could cancer be your fault?" Her voice was so soft it barely had any sound.

"That love of the land? The work? My pride and satisfaction in it? After Dat died, I let it consume me." His voice rasped now, no longer a whisper. "Long hours in the saddle. Putting the work ahead of my wife, the babies. She was so capable, and Mamm and Susanna were there. It never once occurred to me that she would need me to be there, too, and not just to provide."

"Any wife needs her husband with her," Sylvia said help-lessly. How could he imagine a woman wouldn't need him?

"Not like that," he said. "I was there at night, most of the time. But sleeping and eating are different than actually seeing the person you love. And what I didn't see—" He swallowed. "I missed the signs. I was out on the range, watching for signs of predators, for disease, for injury. But with my own wife ... I never saw the weight loss. It was Mamm who finally said something. Lily Anne just made a joke about not having to go on a diet, and off I went, oblivious."

"How could you have known?"

"It wasn't just that. Heartburn, when she'd never had it before. Eating like a bird, yet saying she was full and passing me her plate to finish it." He covered his face with his hands and rubbed it. "A husband who was paying attention would have seen the changes. Maybe looked them up. Added them up. But *neh*, I just saddled up and went out for another day doing the job I loved in the place I loved. But I wasn't looking after the wife I loved. And she—she—"

His shoulders shook. His tears were silent. She heard only shallow gasps of breath amid the soughing of the breeze in the grass beyond.

Her whole being demanded that she move closer, maybe even put her arms around him and give him a hug. The urge was so strong that before she could even name one of the dozens of reasons why she shouldn't, she had slid over and begun rubbing slow, comforting circles on his back.

"How could you have known?" she asked softly, pulling out another handkerchief and handing it to him. He blew his nose and mopped his eyes, and she plucked up her courage. "You're not a doctor. None of us know the signs of cancer until after the fact, do we?"

"I should have—"

"Should, as Mamm often tells us, is an imaginary future that has nothing to do with real life. Should is what other people think you ought to do, not what you actually do. When Lily Anne needed help, you gave it to her, didn't you?"

"But it was too late," he mumbled into the handkerchief. "What good was being by her hospital bed instead of by her side months earlier?"

"You were there when all she had were you and God," she said fiercely. "She didn't tell you. I understand that. But when she did, you did everything you could. Rachel told me at the barn raising that you got your neighbor to take the two of you in his truck all the way to the hospital in Pagosa Springs. And that you slept in the room with her. Talked to the doctors for her." She took a breath. "Gave up your other loves for the one that mattered most."

He sighed. "For all the good it did."

"It did her good. For the time *Gott* gave you, you know it did."

He took a long, shuddering breath. "I've never told anyone the whole story. Not even Mamm, and she was there."

If a tiny spark of joy could be found in such sadness, the fact that he trusted her enough to tell her his deepest shame kindled it in Sylvia's heart. "Sometimes we need someone to listen," she said. "And that coyote down there isn't telling, either."

A grey shadow moved soundlessly across the grass and vanished into the arroyo.

"My ugly secrets are safe with you, is that what you're saying?"

"Love and sacrifice are never ugly. And *ja*, of course anything you say to me is safe." She huffed a laugh. "I have no one to tell your secrets to, anyway. Sharon and Bethany are too busy being *Youngie*. Mamm's mind is filled with running the ranch and what she'll feed the crew next. The only person I've been able to talk to lately is ... your mother."

He moved, a kind of lift of the head that showed his surprise. The brim of his hat tilted up and she saw the gleam of his eyes before it came down again. "I'm glad. For my part, I have to say you're easy to talk to. So easy it all comes spilling out and makes a mess."

"I've had years of practice with messes. Maybe not this kind, though."

"There's always the twins. That ice cream ..."

She had to laugh, and with a quiet delight, she heard him laugh, too. She wanted to hug this moment to her like a treasure and never let it go. But moments have a habit of passing, she reflected, no matter how precious or how awful.

Reluctantly, she slid off the log. "I should be getting back. Mamm is used to my rambles, but she does get worried at night."

"I don't blame her." He rose and waggled his flashlight in one hand. "I'll walk you back."

She would take darkness and coyotes and even thunder and lightning if it meant a few minutes longer with Tobias. Mark and his prospects couldn't even compare.

BENNY WAS SOUND ASLEEP IN THE BUNK ABOVE THAT OF Tobias, curled up like a kitten. Stephen's door was closed, and Mark lay on his back, snoring like a cross-cut saw, as Tobias came out of the bunkhouse bathroom. He adjusted Benny's blankets around him, then knelt by his bed to pray.

Gott in Himmel, thank You for allowing me to lance this boil inside me and finally confess my part in Lily Anne's death. Thank You for sending Sylvia there at just the right time and place. Thank You for her compassion ... and for the fact that she didn't recoil in disgust from me. Help me, Father. I want this hole in my heart to heal, but wanting that feels like a betrayal of my wife. The pain and the memories are all I have of her, and it's hard to give them up. I pray for Your comfort, Lord. Your peace. Help me to wait on You for both those things in patience and willingness. I humbly ask it of You in Jesus' name.

Silently, he rose and leaned on the bunk. They were built against the wall, each one almost like a little room to give the hands as much privacy as possible. At least the mattress was comfortable, and his pillow was one of the two Lily Anne had on their bed at the Four Winds. The skylight set into the ceiling in the wide aisle gave him a fine view of the night sky, sprinkled with so many stars it was like *der Herr* had used a salt shaker. One star alone couldn't produce such a beautiful sight in the oblong of the skylight. It took all of them to proclaim God's power.

As he watched, a meteor streaked across the sky. He hoped Sylvia had seen it, too, from wherever she was in the house.

"Did you see that?" Stephen's shape filled the doorway of the foreman's bedroom. "The shooting star?"

"*Ja*, I did," Tobias said in a voice pitched just as low.

"Come on in here. It's a meteor shower. You can see them through my window."

Tobias stood at the window and marveled at the streaking lights—so quick, so far away they looked tiny, and yet were such a miracle.

"Glad I hadn't fallen asleep yet," Stephen said quietly. "I would hate to have missed it."

"Me too. Thanks for sharing."

"We're going to be family soon. We'll probably be sharing more than this."

Tobias had to smile. "How soon?"

"After your *mamm* and Luke in October. Susanna and I were talking about it this week. We'll talk to the bishop at church and ask when we can come to see him. As far as I'm concerned, tomorrow wouldn't be too soon."

"The sooner the better. Otherwise, with all the weddings coming up at the Circle M, you might have to wait until next year."

"I sure hope you're joking."

He bumped Stephen's shoulder companionably, his gaze on the sky. "Only a little. Adam and Kate ... Zach and Ruby ... Malena and Alden, if they ever get themselves going. If Little Joe schedules one wedding a week, except Thanksgiving, that's all of November right there."

Stephen drew a breath of alarm and Tobias took mercy on him.

"Adam and Kate have decided on December, haven't they? There's a reason he's got Noah and Simeon there almost every day, and he's working long hours on his house. Poor Noah has only got stakes, while Adam has foundation, floor, and studs already."

"And Sim has no house at all. Much to Susan's dismay."

From his brief knowledge of her, Susan Bontrager was the kind of woman who would get what she wanted sooner rather than later, but Tobias didn't say that out loud.

"She's quite the girl," Stephen said. "You're lucky she settled on Simeon before you or I got here. Otherwise it would be one of us bargaining with the King brothers for their time."

Perish the thought. "I feel pretty lucky that Sylvia agreed

to be the twins' nanny. Imagine if things had been different and Susan had the job."

Stephen pretended to shudder. "Can you imagine Susanna and Susan in the Inn simultaneously?"

"Neh," Tobias said flatly. Two such strong personalities would cause sparks to fly—and not the good kind, either.

"I saw her out by the lot line just now," Tobias said, then hastily added, "Sylvia, not Susan. She was walking out to a kind of viewpoint. I was glad I was there. A coyote was hunting not ten yards away."

"I bet you'd have been glad even without the coyote. I like Sylvia. It's *gut* your *Schweschder* is warming up to her."

"Doesn't Susanna like her?" How had Tobias never noticed that? Good grief, did he see nothing but what was right in front of him? Was he that oblivious to everything but his own griefs and worries?

"I don't think they got off on the right foot when we first moved here," Stephen allowed. "I think it was because everyone took it for granted they'd be friends right off the bat. But Sylvia is the kind that warms up to people slowly. She doesn't let people in easily."

Tobias was silent. What did it mean, then, that she had been such a friend, such a comfort to him?

"Maybe that's why she's still single." Stephen lowered his voice, though the snores were still audible in the other room. "Though I have to say that Mark is doing his best to change that."

"She can do better than him," came out of Tobias's mouth before his brain could stop it. "I wish her parents weren't pushing him at her all the time. Seems Josiah would like him to marry her and take the reins when he's ready to hand them over."

"Is that so?" Stephen glanced at him. "And how do you know this?"

"She told me. She's not too happy about it."

"Well, she's a big girl. If she wants him to scram, she just has to tell him."

"I think she's tried, but she's too kind a person to hurt his feelings. Maybe he hasn't got the message. He keeps asking to take her home from singing and she doesn't know what to do."

"She should go home with someone else. That'll send a message." Stephen snorted. "Calvin Yoder, now. Just the man for the job."

He had to be kidding. "I wouldn't wish Calvin Yoder on Susan Bontrager, never mind someone as nice as Sylvia."

"Susan would flay him so bad with the rough side of her tongue he'd never put the pieces back together." Stephen chuckled. "Well, there's only one thing to do."

"What? Ride to the rescue of the boss's daughter?"

"Not me. Are you kidding? Susanna may hold it better, but her tongue is every bit as sharp. *Neh, mei Freind.* You're the last man standing. If anyone is going to get the message across to Mark that she doesn't want him, it'll have to be you."

Tobias gaped at him. "Me? I'm too old for that stuff. And a father besides."

"Whose *Kinner* she is looking after. I'm telling you. Mark may break her down eventually, and then where will we all be?"

"Working for him," Tobias said, feeling a little queasy at the thought. "You don't think she'd give in, do you?"

"No, but thirty is out there on the horizon. Just like you."

"Oh, thanks. You make me feel ancient, you young whippersnapper."

Stephen clapped him on the shoulder. "Just looking out for my family," he said cheerfully. "Don't you have a bed to go to?

If you want a day off to work on your barn Saturday, I'd better see some progress with that pump tomorrow."

Tobias had to chuckle. "Your people skills need work, boss."

"Ah, but my future brother-in-law can handle it. *Guder nacht*, Tobias."

Back at his bunk, Tobias stood listening to the even breathing of his son, and brushed the hair back from his forehead. Benny murmured something and rolled over to face the wall, curling up once more.

His *Kinner* were lucky to have Sylvia to look after them. *He* was lucky. And as he got into bed and gazed up at the underside of Benny's bunk, it stuck in his craw that Mark was chasing her. A woman should have the experience he'd had, of knowing without a doubt that a certain person was the one *Gott* had sent to make his life complete and full of joy.

A woman as good and kind as Sylvia shouldn't have to settle.

❦ 15 ❦

WILD ROSE AMISH INN

Saturday, June 25

TOBIAS HAD to smile as his children raced all over the barn at the Wild Rose Amish Inn, checking to see what had changed in the few days since they'd been inside it. The biggest news was that the family's buggies now stood in the hitching area close to the big sliding door, their rails neatly lined up. No doubt his brother Seth's doing. He had an orderly streak. And then, of course, the *Kinner* had to visit the chickens, who were dust bathing next to the fence around Mamm's garden.

Stephen and Mark had different days off at the Bow K than he did, although everyone had Sunday off. So today, while they worked on the ranch, he could devote an entire day to the barn. His helpers included Luke Hertzler, Hezekiah Zook, and David Yoder, with the possibility of Calvin coming later if the truck delivering a shipment of inventory to Yoder's Variety Store arrived in time. Tobias and Zeke strapped on tool belts. While Luke and David climbed the ladder to the upper floor, Tobias tried to decide which of the dozen tasks he'd take on first. Luke had been carpentering in here all week, which meant the ground floor was completely ready for Rachel's animals, and Zeke had painted it all.

"You've done a nice job with the calving pens and the horse stalls," he said to Zeke. "I'll be sorry to see the first calf spatter on all this white paint."

"It'll wash off," Zeke said. "But it does look clean to start. Nice to see the horses outside and the buggies in here."

"Mamm says Gid and Seth brought them yesterday. That must have been quite the parade here from the Circle M."

Lucy and Murphy, their buggy horses, were out in the newly fenced pasture getting used to their new home. His brothers must have driven the buggies with their own cutting horses tied on behind, so that they could go back to work.

"Reuben will be glad to have the space in his barn again," Zeke said. "Well, best get up there before they start without us."

When they emerged at the top of the ladder, Luke was showing David his punch list. When Tobias and Zeke joined them, Luke handed it to Tobias. "What's up first?"

Tobias didn't hesitate. "Framing in the bunkhouse. Noah marked the floors, and we've got the drawings. The church room is pretty much done except for the trim on the windows."

"Why don't I knock that out first," Zeke suggested, "and join you in a bit for the framing."

"All right. It'll go pretty fast over here with three of us."

By the time Gracie ran down to tell them that Mammi had lunch ready on the verandah, they had the bunkhouse framed in, and sheathed and insulated as well. Since Mamm planned to rent the rooms to hands who didn't have arrangements already made, instead of the dorm style favored by Josiah, they had decided on eight by ten rooms, two on each side of a wide central corridor. They weren't so big, and the bathroom and common area, of course, were shared, but big enough for a double bed and a place to hang up their clothes. Calvin showed up around one o'clock, and with a guest from the Inn joining them, the work went even faster. One thing about Calvin—he might be the most socially inept person Tobias had ever met, but give him a task and he got it done almost before you could turn around.

Toward the end of the day, Tobias could smell the scent of a beef roast wafting down the slope from the Inn's outdoor barbecue. "You've all done good work," he told his crew, speaking *Englisch* for the benefit of Rob, the Inn's guest. "I hope you'll let us give you supper, at least, to say thanks."

"Suits me," Calvin said.

"But being Saturday night, we won't stay too late," Dave added. "Zeke, what about you?"

"My brother might like a day off from looking at my ugly mug across the table," Zeke said.

"You just want to sample Rachel's cooking," Luke teased.

"If it's as good as her breakfasts," Rob said, "I might join your crew every day."

"You'd sure be welcome, if you want to give up your vacation," Tobias said, shedding his belt and batting sawdust off his shirt sleeves. "Every pair of hands makes the work go faster, and we're not far from being finished now."

"I'm a contractor these days, managing my own crews, but I got my start swinging a hammer for my dad," Rob said. "It feels good to work these muscles again."

Noah had plumbed in a sink in the tack room, and they baptized it when they washed up. Luke led the way up the slope, while Calvin and David brought up the rear, bickering about how late they were going to stay.

Finally Tobias rolled his eyes and told them, "My *Kinner* need to be in bed by seven, and we like a little Bible reading time before that, so if you boys head home around six, that would suit us fine."

"See?" Calvin bumped his brother's shoulder and made him stagger. "Told you." He galloped off up the slope as though that would hurry his dinner.

Dave rubbed his shoulder. "Is Sylvia still looking after your *Kinner*?"

"It's only been two weeks. Did you think they'd frighten her off so soon?"

"They're a handful."

Tobias chose not to be offended. "Maybe, but they always mean well. And Sylvia is *gut* with them. They really like her."

"I hear they're not the only ones."

He glanced at David curiously. "What do you mean?"

"I was talking with Bethany at the store the other day. She says Mark Steiner is pretty sweet on Sylvia, even if she is older than him."

He made her sound like she was forty if she was a day. "I suppose Bethany would know. I'm out on the range most of the time, so stuff like that tends to go right by me."

"Is he giving her a ride home tomorrow?"

"How would I know?" Tobias caught himself before his irritation showed. "I'm not one to gossip about people who work for me."

David took the reproof in stride, and without any more questions, headed for the chairs set out on the grass on the south side of the house. As Tobias walked up, Rob was talking to the lady painters, who would be leaving on Monday.

"Is Rachel cooking for Rob as well as you folks?" The taller one sounded plaintive. "Oh my, that smells so good."

"Greta, you know the policy. Evening meals are on our own," her companion said in a low voice.

"Rob gave us a hand with the carpentry today," Tobias said with a smile. "Feeding our crew is the least we can do to thank them."

"I have an idea." Greta vanished into the house, and a moment later returned with a sheet of thick paper about two feet square. "What if we paid for our dinner with this?"

It was a painting of the Inn, taken from the east side where the patio was, complete with wild roses and even chickens, painted in such meticulous detail it looked like a photograph. Tobias whistled with admiration. "You surely don't want to give that up. It's beautiful."

"I can paint another from my reference shots. Do you think your mother would like it?"

Susanna was peering over his shoulder by now. "I don't know if she will, but I do. Greta, it's wonderful. You are more than welcome to supper." She took the picture with reverent hands. "Mom always makes way more than anybody can eat."

Supper was a congenial meal. Mamm was thrilled with the painting and pressed second helpings on Greta and her friend. And when Dave and Calvin headed off through the pines that divided the properties, and Mamm, Susanna, and Luke took the dishes in to be washed, Zeke and Tobias sat on a couple of the folding chairs in the low rays of the sun and stretched their boots out into the grass.

"That was a fine meal," Zeke said. "I don't think my work matched my compensation, but I sure feel satisfied."

"I'm pretty satisfied with your work," Tobias told him with

a smile. "*Denki*, Zeke. I know you took time away from your own to help with mine."

"I needed a little time away. *Mei Bruder* is not so talkative lately. Figured I'd get better conversation over here."

"Something on his mind?" Goats, probably. Or some difficulty with a shipment of cheeses.

"Woman trouble," Zeke said darkly.

The train of Tobias's thoughts abruptly derailed. "Willard? Woman trouble?" From what he'd heard in the months they'd lived here, Willard Zook hadn't had woman trouble in thirty years.

"*Ja*. He even roped her mother into helping him. The other day he finally rustled up the courage to ask her if she'd mind courting." He snorted. "That was how he put it. If she'd *mind*. Not exactly a salesman, my brother."

"What did she say?" Tobias ran through a mental list of the widows and various other single ladies in the district, but couldn't remember Willard even speaking to one of them other than the greeting everyone gave each other after church.

"She turned him down." Zeke sighed. "And now it's all I can do to get a word out of him. He says more to the bees than he does to me."

"I'm sorry to hear that. Bees?"

"We have some hives, up at one end of the Miller parcel. He's *gut* with bees. Introduced her to them. He's got to be far gone to do that. Bees are particular about who they associate with."

In the blink of an eye, a bedtime conversation he'd had with Benny the other night about bees and an errand on which Kathryn Keim had sent her daughter connected in his brain with something akin to an electrical charge. "Are you talking about Sylvia Keim? Willard asked Sylvia if he could court her?"

"*Ja*, didn't I say? Nicest young lady in the world. Faithful, too. Bees liked her. But I don't know what he was thinking. He's past courting age. Leave that to young people like you and me."

Zeke was two years younger than his brother. Did he have designs on Sylvia, too? Tobias's thoughts felt like a flock of starlings, all flapping and squawking at once.

"But I suppose a woman knows her own mind," Zeke went on. "I hope he hasn't scared her off. Now that the bees have been introduced to her and your *Kinner*, it would be nice to see them once in a while. They ran up to our place all the time when they lived here."

"It's only for the summer." But Tobias hardly knew what he was saying. Sylvia hadn't said a word to him about it. Here he was, spilling his guts to her the other night, and not a word about this in return.

She told you about Mark. So what if she kept Willard's offer to herself?

Mark might have some things going for him, like youth and skills and ambition. But Willard was established, with a home the church met in and a longstanding business. Granted, he was far too old for her. Some days Tobias felt fifty ... but Willard actually was, if not more. Still, he was a better prospect than Mark.

But if she hadn't told him about it the other night, did that mean she was having second thoughts about Willard's offer?

What does it matter to you, you sorry Narr? What Josiah Keim's daughter does with her life has nothing to do with you unless it concerns your children.

It did concern the children. Sort of—if she up and married Willard before summer's end. But how likely was that? He didn't know. And it bothered him not to know. It bothered him that he had opened up to her and she hadn't done the same.

Zeke got up and wished him a good night. "See you all tomorrow at Eichers'."

Tobias murmured something and sat there, staring at the pines without really seeing them at all. It wasn't until Susanna came out to say the family was waiting for him in the sitting room for Bible reading that he came back to himself.

He followed her in. Read the verses in his turn. Took the twins to their room, heard their prayers, and kissed them good night. And when it came time to say his own prayers, he waited a long time on his knees to feel the peace that usually filled his soul.

But tonight, it seemed, peace was as elusive as any bird in flight.

Sunday, June 26

Since the Eicher ranch was away at the far end of the valley, it meant that most of the folks in the east district had to have breakfast and be hitched up to leave by seven at the latest. This morning, Sylvia felt the absence of Tobias and the twins across the big dining table at the Bow K as she looked up after grace and reached for the bowl of biscuits. Those two only been here a couple of weeks and already it felt as though they'd be sitting opposite her, chattering away about plans for the day, forever.

But a person couldn't count on forever, could they? Only with God could you do that. With people, she supposed, you could be glad for the days you had them, and miss them on the days when you didn't.

She climbed into the buggy with her parents, while Mark

took Sharon and Bethany in his. Normally he'd have Pete and Danny with him, but today being the first church Sunday since their departure, he wanted company and Sylvia made certain she wasn't anywhere near while they got that all sorted out. Funny how riding to church in the morning with a single man didn't make the same statement that going home with him at night did. But then, she supposed, on the way to church, you were supposed to be thinking about receiving a message from God and preparing your heart and spirit. Not thinking about the man beside you and wondering if he was going to try to kiss you when he stopped the buggy.

Not that she could think about kissing anyone but Tobias. Mark? Willard? Her mind shuddered away.

She was happy enough to sit in church knowing Mark was off somewhere on the men's side toward the rear. And, as on any church Sunday, it was normal to shake hands out in the sunshine in the interval between the last hymn and the invitation to the fellowship meal. She made a point of not avoiding the Zook brothers, too. She might not welcome a courtship from Willard, but he was still her friend. She offered her hand with a smile first to Zeke and then to Willard, and inquired after the bees.

"They're well." Willard's face brightened at the sight of her, which was so sweet that she was glad she'd made a point of coming over. "They send their regards."

She had to laugh. "I hope you let them know that they're welcome on the Bow K. The twins and I will be glad to see them. I've already told my family and the hands that any mistreatment of honeybees is strictly forbidden."

"Did you?" Zeke raised his eyebrows.

"I surely did, yesterday at breakfast, before everyone scattered to their work."

"Glad to hear it," Willard said. "My brother was over to the Inn to help out in the barn yesterday. Says they got the bunkhouse roughed in and the trim completed in the church room."

Sylvia squashed a spurt of dissatisfaction at being left out of such doings, even if her only contribution would have been picking up nails. Yes, she'd been happy to work on the quilt she was piecing, but still. The girls had gone to town shopping and it had been a very quiet day. She'd sewed seams thinking more about how she'd teach Gracie to stitch them than actually focusing on the snowball design she'd been so happy to start after Easter.

"I'm glad you made so much progress," she said. "I was working on a quilt. I'm going to teach Gracie how to use the treadle machine, so I thought I had better get reacquainted with my own first." As if she'd heard her name, Gracie ran up to hug Sylvia around the waist. "Hallo, *Liewi*. Willard and Zeke were saying the bees missed us."

"I know," the little girl said. "They came over to the roses on our fence and I heard them buzzing." She lowered her voice to a hum. *"Hmmmweemmissyouuum."*

Delighted, Sylvia giggled. "That's exactly how it sounded at our place, too. I missed you as well."

"Did you? We'll be back tonight. Dat said."

"Zeke, there's Barbara King," Willard said. "I want to inquire after Aendi Annie." He nodded, and with a smile for Gracie, he and Zeke went on their way.

Fraa Eicher called them all a few minutes later, and it seemed natural for Gracie to go in with her for the fellowship meal. To Sylvia's relief, Mark and the Eicher boys were holding court with the girls at a table near the back of the big living room, now transformed into a dining room with rows of benches and tables. As if her gaze were a bee and Tobias the hive filled with honey, she found him and Benny near the windows, where Rachel Miller and Luke sat with them, along with Susanna and Stephen.

Once they had piled their plates with ham, cheese, and pickle sandwiches (for Sylvia) and peanut butter spread (for Gracie) and added chips and red coleslaw, Gracie said, "Come on," and pulled her by the hand across the room to join them.

Sylvia would never in a hundred years have been so forward, but with Gracie managing the situation, the family quite naturally slid over on their benches to make room for them both. Luke twinkled at Gracie. "This is more like it. Suppers at the Inn aren't the same without you."

She twinkled back, with a mighty swallow of peanut butter and marshmallow. "I miss home, but at the ranch, we're with Dat and Stephen and I like that."

"I did a little quilting yesterday," Sylvia told her. "Maybe we can start your quilt tomorrow, after we do the washing."

"*Gut!*" Gracie exclaimed. "I've been waiting and waiting."

Sylvia's gaze flickered to Tobias, who was smothering a smile with food. "It's been a terrible long time," she agreed. "Four whole days since we got your fabric."

"What design are you going to make?" Susanna asked her niece.

Gracie looked at Sylvia for help. "A nine-patch on point, with two borders," Sylvia supplied. "And she's going to be brave and try a bed-sized quilt."

"For my bed," Gracie clarified, in case they might think it was for a big adult bed.

"Big pieces with lots of nice straight seams," Rachel said with a nod. "A *gut* place to start."

"And after you make it, you can bring it outside when we go camping," Benny said. "Maybe even this week."

"Quilts take longer to make than that," Gracie said scornfully. "We'll use the bedrolls."

"This again?" Tobias asked them. "What is this fascination with sleeping out on the lawn?"

"It will be fun." Benny took a huge bite of his sandwich and spoke through it. "You and Sylvia can come with us."

The little boy looked mystified when everyone laughed. Sylvia took pity on him. "I can't, *Liewi*, but your Dat might enjoy it."

"Why can't you?" Gracie looked from her to her father.

"Because I'm *dei Vater*, but Sylvia isn't *mei Fraa*," Tobias explained gently. "Only a wife could join us in the tent. It wouldn't be fitting otherwise."

"Oh. Well," she said in a tone that waved away this irrelevant detail, "next year, then."

Was it possible for a face to actually catch fire from within? The heat of embarrassment beat in Sylvia's cheeks and probably right up past her hairline and under her *Kapp*. She didn't know whether to run away or just expire on the spot and be carried out.

"Tobias, can you get the water jug?" Rachel asked calmly, and in his rising to get it from farther down the table, the awful moment staggered past. By the time he handed it to his mother, Susanna had launched into some other subject that flowed by Sylvia like rushing water, all sound and no sense.

She was so thankful to escape outside without any further disasters.

Normally Sylvia spoke with a few people after lunch, enjoyed watching and listening to others, and then was relieved when Dat went to catch the horse and it was time to go home with her parents. Today, every moment crept by on lame legs. Mamm was far too interested in catching up with the other ranchers' wives, and while Sylvia tried to look interested, too, all she could think of was the blessed quiet of her room at home. The twins would be with their father, and she could hide in peace.

But there was no hiding at church. You couldn't even lock yourself in the bathroom, because there was always a line standing outside and it was only considerate to be as quick as you could.

Finally Sylvia took refuge in Connie Eicher's enormous garden, walking around its perimeter and pretending to be interested in the bean and pea teepees, the rows of baby lettuce and spinach, and the tomatoes that were so heavily fertilized that they were practically growing on horse manure alone. Then again, when they only had three months to produce, every little bit helped.

"Sylvia."

Her knees nearly buckled at the sound of Tobias's voice. If he wanted to talk about that awful moment at the table, or worse, apologize for his *Dochder*—

"What are you doing out here?" He stopped a little distance away and gazed into the garden as if to figure out what seemed to interest her.

Little did he know that it interested her only as a shield. And it had clearly failed her.

"I'm always interested in how Connie manages her plants," she said in a voice that was, thankfully, fairly steady. "Mamm and I have to grow our tomatoes in pots in the sun room."

"They're probably safer from bugs there," he said. "Sylvia, I want to apologize for Gracie. She didn't realize she was embarrassing you."

I bet she did, the little rascal. I haven't forgotten what your mother told me about what she and Benny are up to.

"It's all right. I guess at that age, having your favorite people in the tent all together would seem like a *gut* plan."

He chuckled. "In five years they won't want their old dad in the tent with them—they'll be packing their buddy bunch in there and chattering long past midnight."

"They grow so fast," she said. "You have to take your moments when you can. Are you going to let them camp out?"

"It seems harmless enough," he admitted. "I don't see the romance and the adventure in it, but clearly they do. I'm not much looking forward to sleeping out there with them. Bedrolls are comfortable in comparison to a long day of riding and roping. Compared to a normal day of work, not so much."

"You'll be all the more thankful for your own bunk."

"That I will. Listen, Sylvia—"

On the far side of the fence about fifty feet away, Rhoda nickered and Sylvia heard her father's low whistle to call her in.

"Dat is hitching up the buggy. I'd best be going, Tobias."

"Wait— I just wondered— You're not staying for the singing?"

"*Neh*, I was going to go home with them."

"Oh." He seemed puzzled. "I thought Mark was giving you a ride home afterward."

"He asked me. But since he's been with my cousins most of the day, I have a feeling he's given up."

Tobias lifted his head and for the briefest moment, their eyes met before Sylvia's gaze skittered past him. Dat had caught Rhoda and was leading her to the gate.

"Well ... instead of going home with your parents, maybe you'd like to go for a ride with the twins and me? If we take the long way home by the foothills, we might see a moose in the marsh. The *Kinner* have never seen one."

"And how do you know about moose in the marsh?"

"Calvin told me, while we were working on the bunkhouse. That kid is a fountain of information about local wildlife."

"That's because he and his father are hunters," Sylvia said wryly. "The only calendar Calvin is interested in is the one that comes with the deer and elk hunting regulations. All the old-timers in the valley are like that—even Willard and Zeke, who wouldn't hurt a fly otherwise."

"Anyway, we'd be glad if you'd come along," Tobias said, roping her back on topic. "We wouldn't get you home much later than if you went with your folks."

Why was he doing this? Was he just trying to make up for embarrassing her at lunch? Was she a complete and utter fool for wanting to go, no matter what his reasons were?

If you don't go, you'll spend the whole afternoon wishing you had. So why not go, even if you're letting yourself in for an afternoon of the finest torture a woman can know?

She was all kinds of a fool. So be it. "*Ja*, I'd like to. I've only seen a moose twice before in my life. The third time might be the charm."

❦ 16 ❧

SYLVIA KNEW she was in for it when the twins scrambled into
the rear of the buggy, leaving the seat on Tobias's left for her.
The stifled giggles in the back did not help her peace of mind,
either. But she had walked into this with her eyes open, so she
would go through with it.

Tobias didn't seem to notice anything—or he was making a
point of ignoring it. Either way, she could only be grateful.
Instead, he talked about Lucy the horse and how good it felt
to be driving his own buggy again.

She realized belatedly that this would have been the family
buggy in New Mexico. And that a ghost was probably sitting
beside him as well as her more substantial self. But as the twins
chattered behind them and she pointed out to them the land-
marks she'd known all her life, her awareness of the space Lily
Anne once held seemed to fade.

They left homes and farms behind and took the country
road that wound through the hills westward. "How many kinds
of flowers can you name?" she asked the *Kinner*. Montana was
certainly at its peak in the warmth of the June sun. The twins

178

named the ones they knew on the roadsides—wild roses, of course, but also lupine, Queen Anne's Lace, and brown-eyed Susans. Sylvia pointed out the ones they would come to love as much as she did—bachelor buttons, larkspur, and fireweed.

"Country folks call it fireweed because they believe it only grows where there's been a fire." She pointed at a wave of pink and red flowers and an old, blackened stump on a hillside.

"Reminds me of that verse about beauty for ashes," Tobias said.

"Isaiah, isn't it? *Beauty for ashes, the oil of joy for mourning, the garment of praise for the spirit of heaviness; that they might be called trees of righteousness, the planting of the Lord.*"

"*Ja*, that's it. What a *gut* memory you have."

She smiled. "I like to think of His people being the planting of the Lord here in the Siksika. Dat used to have us memorize verses during the summer, to keep our reading up." She glanced behind her. "Maybe we should add that to the spelling words."

Benny said hastily, "How far is the marsh?"

"About a mile. But it is the middle of the afternoon. Moose like the early morning and twilight. We might not see one, but we could see ducks and maybe a muskrat or a white egret or two."

The marsh lay under the pine forest in a low spot, and ran close enough to the road that you could see across the quarter mile or so to where some of the pines actually stood in the water.

"Later in the summer it will probably dry out a little, but this is the best time," she told the children. "Shall we ask Dat to tie Lucy near that cattle guard?"

It was clear that the acres of pine forest stretching up over the hill and into the distance belonged to somone's allotment, but they wouldn't mind them stopping in the clearing. The children pulled off their Sunday shoes and socks and tumbled out. Sylvia barely had time to remind them to be careful where they put their feet when they were scrambling down toward the marsh.

"They probably won't see anything but frogs," Tobias remarked, joining her to walk around where the slope fell a little more gently. "Or whatever lives in cattails besides mosquito larvae."

"Nothing that can hurt them, I don't think. Most everything but a moose will avoid being seen by humans."

He offered her a hand to step down from a granite boulder and she took it. A tingle ran up her arm at its warmth and strength. *Goodness*. She let go.

"Have you been down here?"

"Not since I was a child," she said, hoping he hadn't seen her reaction. "It's too far for a boy to drive a courting buggy, and none of the *Gmay* live along this road, so we don't travel on it for church. Mostly, it's *Englisch* people taking the scenic route, or hunters going up on the allotments."

"Ach, look at those two." Tobias shook his head. "Up to their ankles in mud."

"It's cold," Gracie complained loudly enough for them to hear. "What if I step on a toad?"

"Toads fall asleep in the cold," Sylvia told her, making her way gingerly down the grassy slope. Clumps of sedge grass dotted the smooth ground, and Gracie was right. While it had dried out some, it was squishy. She should have thought about her Sunday shoes.

"Sylvia." Tobias's voice was hushed. "Benny. Gracie. Look over there." He pointed.

Sylvia drew in a breath. A shape flickered among the deadheads and cattails. A very large shape.

"Children," she said softly. "Don't move." Gracie stopped hauling up her dress and clutched it in her hands. "Look to your left."

Benny's eyes went wide. "I see it."

"What?" Gracie was about five feet away from him. "What do you see?" She took a couple of steps toward him. "Benny, I'm sinking."

But he ignored her. "Look. It's a moose!"

"Where?" She took one step toward him.

"Gracie, stop!" Tobias commanded.

She did, still straining to see what everyone else could, and had somehow managed to sink six inches. The wadded-up dress was soaked in her hands.

Sylvia gasped. "Muskeg!" She toed off her shoes and reached under her own dress to yank down her black stockings. Kicking them off, she slid down the slope, only half conscious of rocks rolling under her heels.

"Sylvia!" Tobias shouted. "What's wrong?"

"They're standing in muskeg," she flung over her shoulder. "We've got to get them out."

The moose gave a great snort at her movement and with a huge heave, propelled itself out of the deeper water and into the shallows. It shook itself and galloped into the pines. In a less dangerous moment, she might have marveled at how something so big could vanish so completely. But now was not the time.

Out farther than his sister, Benny had somehow sunk to the waist. "I can't get out!" He was already in tears. "Sylvia, it's all mud. I'm stuck!"

"I'm coming, Benny. Gracie, can you move your feet?"

"Ewwww," she wailed. She yanked a knee skyward, which only put more weight on the other foot. She sank four inches. "Dat!" She began to cry.

The thin surface layer of brackish, peaty water was lapping at the buttons on Benny's shirt now.

Barefoot, his face a mask of panic, Tobias ran out on the deceptively smooth, mossy ground.

"Get Gracie!" Sylvia shouted. "Move fast so you don't sink."

She snatched up a thick branch that had probably lain here undisturbed for a hundred years. "Benny! Grab hold. Kick your feet like you're swimming and the mud will release you."

She felt herself sink into the soft, deceitful black mud that looked so solid under its shallow skin of water. It would support a person just until they got out far enough, when the surface would break and they'd find themselves in thick, viscous ooze that sucked them in the more they tried to get out. Gracie hadn't been wrong about the freezing cold—ice lay somewhere far below despite the balmy afternoon.

Sobbing, Benny grabbed the branch with both hands. She backed up one step, two, three ... hoping all the while she was moving toward solid ground. As she went, she pulled the branch closer, hand over hand. With a reluctant slurp, the muskeg released him. One more haul on the branch broke it, but she was close enough to grab his hand.

And realized a moment too late that she herself had gone in up to her knees, the hems of her dress soaked and black.

"Benny, I'm going to toss you toward your *dat* as hard as I can. Ready?"

Oof, but he was heavy. She took him by his collar and the seat of his pants and tossed him as hard as she could toward Tobias, who had just deposited Gracie on the bank. Benny landed spreadeagled in the shallow water, a great wave of weed and bits of peat washing up as Tobias grabbed him with both hands and dragged him out.

Now she had to free herself. The branch might be broken, but she could use it like a clumsy, oversized walking stick. All she wanted to do was run, but she'd never get out that way. With slow, even pressure upward, battling her instincts, she lifted her feet one at a time against the suck of the muskeg, making slow, slow progress until it consented to let her go. No hurry. No sudden movements that would put any more weight on the layers of rotting mud.

The branch hit solid footing. She slogged out of the mud looking like the children—black to the thighs and with smudges and gobs of it all over her Sunday dress and apron.

Who cared? She collapsed on the bank, gasping with relief and gabbling words of thanks to *der Herr*. "I'm so sorry," she managed, her voice wobbling. "I didn't know it was muskeg. I never would have brought them here if—"

Tobias wiped his face, and a handprint of black mud slid toward his ear. "Great heavenly days, I'd have gone plunging in there after Benny and wound up sinking before I could even reach him."

"What—is—muskeg?" Benny smeared his face trying to wipe away the tears.

"It's mud and it's stinky," his sister informed him, trying to scrape the stuff off her legs with the blades of her hands.

"It is," Sylvia agreed, half laughing, half crying. "It's boggy stuff that has rotted so that it's firm on top and gooey underneath, like a half-baked cake."

Gracie's face contorted in disgust at her lack of progress with the mud.

"You can get pretty far if you're moving fast enough not to break the surface," she finished. "But once you do ..."

"You start to sink," Tobias finished. "I can't think about it. I'm going to have nightmares for weeks."

"What would we have done without you?" Gracie said in a small voice, giving up and cuddling against Sylvia's side.

"Probably not gone in the water," she said wryly. The mud on her legs was drying already in the sun. What a mess the buggy was going to be.

"Not even their mother could keep them out of it." He wrung out Gracie's dress, trying to sluice some of the mud off her without much success. "But she'd have done a better job of cleaning them up than this."

Sylvia's hands faltered on Benny's shirttails, where she was squeezing out muddy water.

"Mamm would have seen that branch, too, wouldn't she?" he asked Gracie, who only looked puzzled at a question she couldn't possibly answer. "Not like your dad, who's never seen muskeg in his life. Well, we won't forget it in a hurry."

"I wish we had a washtub in the back of the buggy," Sylvia said, trying to make the conversation seem normal. "We could have filled it with water and had a good wash."

"We'll have to make do with the garden hose once we get home." Tobias got up, and the two of them hauled the children to their feet. What a sorry sight they made! But at least no one had drowned. Or been rushed by that moose, which would have had the same result.

Lily Anne would have known to use the branch, would she? *Hmph*. Sylvia stalked up the slope, Benny's hand glued to hers with mud, and collected her shoes and stockings. Not that she deserved any thanks for bringing them out here when it wasn't safe. All the same, was it too much to ask for just a little thank-you that she had remembered what to do to save them?

THE HORROR OF THOSE MOMENTS COVERED TOBIAS LIKE A cloud on their uncomfortable, stinking, sticky journey home. All the charm of the day had evaporated in the face of the children's narrow escape from death. When they reached the Bow K, he tied Lucy to the guest hitching rail next to a buggy he recognized and one he didn't, and the four of them hightailed it over to the garden hose.

Thank goodness Stephen and Mark were still at Eichers', otherwise he'd never hear the end of it. But Josiah and Kathryn were home, and worse, they had Sunday afternoon company. Naomi and Reuben Miller and Mamm and Luke were drinking lemonade out on the wide, old-fashioned porch, and all of them came to the railing to gawk at them on the grass beside Kathryn's peony bushes, hosing themselves down.

"What on earth...?" Kathryn couldn't even find the words.

"What happened?" Mamm managed, her eyes huge.

"That looks like—" Josiah began.

"Muskeg," Sylvia said grimly. She'd got Gracie clean, and was hosing her own dress and legs. Black mud cascaded from both in rivulets. "That marsh a mile past the intersection, where the hunters park at the bottom of the allotment."

"You took the *Kinner* down there?" Kathryn said, her tone spiraling upward. "It's dangerous!"

"I didn't remember until it was too late," Sylvia said simply, handing Tobias the running hose. "I haven't been out there since I was a child."

"And I'll guarantee that was the twins' only visit." Tobias got to work on his son.

With the resilience of children, their near-death escape was fast transforming into an epic tale. Both of them talked at once, regaling the grownups with how they'd sunk into the mud, how Sylvia had used the branch, how she'd thrown Benny through the air so that he belly-flopped in the shallows. But despite these indignities, they'd outwitted the muskeg and emerged triumphant.

"And we're never, ever going down there again, even if there's a dozen moose," Gracie concluded. "Sylvia, I'm cold."

"*Kumm mit*, you two, and we'll get you into the bathtub. Otherwise, we're going to be smelling that mud for the rest of the day."

They ran inside and the door closed behind her. Tobias hosed himself down, the cold water somehow much friendlier than the water in the marsh.

"Guess you could do with a shower, too," Onkel Reuben remarked. "Never seen anything like it. I'd forgotten we had a stretch of muskeg around here."

"I'm half tempted to make a danger sign and take it up there," Tobias said. He shut off the water and gazed down at his soaked pants. "I came out of this better than Benny, at any rate."

"That's because Sylvia went in after him, sounds like," Kathryn pointed out. "That's another dress for barn work. She'll never get the stains out of it."

"A dress is a small price to pay for the children's safety," Mamm said. "I wonder she knew what to do. I've never even seen muskeg, or could identify it if I did."

"I just thought it was a pond," Tobias said. How could people forget such a danger was lying in wait for the unsuspecting? "But you don't realize it's not until you're out on the muskeg, and it starts to wiggle like jelly, and then you're sinking. Beats me how Sylvia didn't recognize it."

"I hope you're not blaming *mei Dochder* for this." Josiah's gaze was as calm as his tone, but Tobias had heard it often enough to rein in his emotions.

"Of course not," he said gruffly. "I'm glad she knew what to do once she let the kids go down there and we found out what it was."

"Tobias," Mamm said. Her tone was not so calm. "You are their father. The responsibility for letting those children go anywhere is yours."

"Do you think I don't know that?" he exploded in disbelief. "I'm going to have nightmares about Benny's face as he sank into that stuff. Do you think I'm happy about this whole situation? That I—" His throat closed and he spun blindly away.

The next thing he knew, Luke Hertzler had his arm around his shoulders and was guiding him across the yard to the barn. Up the stairs to the bunkhouse. Luke turned on the shower and somehow, through his self-recrimination and shame and rage, Tobias got himself undressed and under the hot water, where it beat down on him.

When he came out into the common area, clothed and in his right mind, Luke was sitting on the beat-up sofa that was far more comfortable than it looked. "I'm sorry," he said to the man who had loved his mother for years.

"You don't need to apologize to me," Luke said. "Josiah, maybe, for those remarks about his daughter."

With a sigh, Tobias sank onto the other end of the sofa. "We were having such a nice time, too. What an awful way to end a Sunday."

"It's not over yet. Kathryn's asked us all to stay for dinner."

Great. His cloud of witnesses could sit around the table and judge him for being a bad parent. "Josiah must think I'm a poor specimen, blaming the woman who saved my *Kinner* for getting them into the situation in the first place."

"From what I understood, she didn't remember it was muskeg, or recognize it right away. Do you remember where the whirlpools were twenty years ago in the Chama River?"

He remembered swimming in the river that cut through the ranch. Sunny summer days and pranks on his little brothers and pulling trout out of it to take home to Mamm. "There are whirlpools?"

"Yep," Luke said. "A kayaker lost his life last summer. As the *Englisch* say, I rest my case."

Tobias was silent. "Point taken."

"A man could go a long way before he found a woman like that," he mused.

"*This* man will go a long way to avoid a marsh, for sure and certain."

"How many young women can say they saved a child's life?" Luke was persistent, Tobias would say that for him. "Or made friends with bees? Or have such a way with *Kinner*? Not many, I'd say."

"Luke, whatever you're getting at, you're wasting your breath. I'm not going to court Sylvia. I never was. And after today, I'm pretty sure I never will." When his future stepfather said nothing, he went on, "I know myself. I'm a one-woman man. And if that means I bring up the twins alone, then I'll do the best I can, with *Gott*'s help."

"Even if *Gott* sends someone to be a helpmeet for you?"

That was a little presumptuous of him. How could he know what *Gottes wille* was for Tobias? "How would I know that?"

"Presumably you were pretty convinced of it the first time."

For a man who didn't say much, Luke was good at nailing a point to the wall and making it stick.

"I haven't felt that way with S—with anyone." Appreciating a woman's smile was not the same as recognizing your partner in *Gottes wille*. "Sylvia is *gut* with the *Kinner*, I'll grant you. And if she's willing to look after them, then I'm reasonably confident they're safe with her. As long as there's no muskeg involved. But more than that ... *neh*. I've got nothing to give a woman. She deserves better."

"Sounds like there are one or two who might agree with you."

Ouch. Why did people keep saying that?

"I'd best get back to Rachel." Luke slapped his knees and rose. "There's nothing quite as warming to the soul as seeing them three mothers in Israel talking up a storm while they put together a dinner fit for a king. We are blessed in our women, Tobias Miller."

"*Ja*, I know."

But Luke had already ambled out the door. Tobias heard him speaking to someone at the bottom of the steps, and then the barn door closed. He scooped up a pair of pants and a shirt for Benny, as well as some underwear and socks, slid on his boots, and followed him down. When he emerged into the yard, Luke had already reached the house. He held the door for Sylvia, now wearing a lavender dress and a black kitchen apron, and the two of them disappeared inside.

Never mind what *she* was wearing. Tobias set off to find his son, who he devoutly hoped had managed to stay clean enough to make it worthwhile putting fresh clothes on him.

IT WAS all Sylvia could do to keep a pleasant smile pasted on as Luke let her precede him into the house. Then, even though she should offer Mamm, Rachel, and Naomi some help in the kitchen, she couldn't face it. Not for a few minutes. Not until she could control the tears that were even now stinging her eyes.

She escaped to her room and closed the door, then sat on the bed, gazing sightlessly out the window, and let them flow.

He had hurt her almost beyond bearing, and he didn't even know it. She had gone out to the bunkhouse to collect some fresh clothes for Benny, and was halfway up the stairs when she realized Tobias and Luke were talking about her.

Blaming the woman who saved my Kinner for getting them into the situation in the first place.

She had to face it. Tobias Miller would likely forgive her for allowing his children near that muskeg, but he would never forget, just like he would never forget Lily Anne.

I'm not going to court Sylvia. I never was. And after today, I'm pretty sure I never will.

How was she going to bear the slashing pain of this final rejection? He'd rather live the rest of his life as a single father than marry her. Would rather face old age alone than share it with her. Surely death itself could not be worse than feeling her dreams curl up and die, her heart constrict as love took the death blow.

She had to look the truth in the face. She couldn't nourish this unrequited love any longer. She had to let it die.

She had to summon the strength to look away from everything she delighted in noticing about him—his rare laugh, his love for his children, his bravery in taking any job offered, no matter how humble, to provide for them. The way he adjusted his hat. The way he walked. The way he kissed.

She groaned and scrubbed her face with her hands. And yet more tears kept coming, overflowing into her fingers until she sobbed—silently, so that no one passing her door could hear.

I'm a one-woman man.

That was the worst of it. Surely, after that kiss, he knew on some level how she felt about him. And yet he could tell Luke that it meant nothing. That he would rather be faithful to the memory of his wife than to embrace the reality of another woman's love.

A woman, Sylvia forced herself to admit, who would marry him on any terms. Even those. Even knowing that his heart would never belong to her completely. Oh yes, she would. If he opened that door right now and came in with a proposal on his lips, she would say yes without hesitation.

Have you no self-respect?

Maybe not at this moment. But she'd best learn some pretty quick. She had to lift up her head, go downstairs, and smile ... and not for one moment let anyone suspect that she loved Tobias Miller. Her breath soughed out of her in a long sigh, and she found a handkerchief in the nightstand to dry the evidence of her tears and blow her nose. That was the hard part, wasn't it? Maybe she could find a way to pretend until pretense became reality and she no longer cared. But that seemed like such a betrayal of love it hurt nearly as much as his words had.

People often felt sorry for her, being nearly thirty and with no hope of a husband. She'd known that for some time. But it was worse when they overlooked her altogether. Did every *Gmay* have an old maid who became such a fixture they took her for granted?

Better that than what they'd say if they knew her feelings.

There goes Sylvia Keim. She was in love with Tobias Miller, you know, but he only wanted her for his children's nanny. Such a waste, isn't it? If there was anyone born to be a mother, it was Sylvia. And now it's too late. She'll die an old maid.

Her hand spasmed, crumpling the handkerchief into a ball.

Was that really her only option? Staying single every bit as firmly as Tobias? Or was there another option open to her? That would stave off the gossip she was sure traveled the Amish grapevine whenever it occurred to someone to think of her?

There were two options, in fact.

She'd just admitted to herself that she would marry Tobias even if he didn't love her. Well then, what if she turned that admission on its head? Could she marry someone else even if she didn't love him?

Could she be Fraa Steiner?

Sylvia was no fool. She could see pretty clearly what life would be like with Mark. For sure and certain, Dat and Mamm thought highly of him and it would please them no end to see her settled on the ranch, her future secure. Mark would take over running the cattle business, and in time her parents would move into the *Daadi Haus* they'd build, and she and Mark would fill the big house with children and probably a dog and maybe a couple of cats who would start out as barn cats and eventually wheedle their way inside.

What a perfect life. What a shame that while on the outside it made the picture of prosperity, on the inside she would be struggling constantly to bear up under his lack of true respect for her. She didn't know if it was just her, or if he felt that way about any woman who caught his attention. But lack of respect bred all kinds of problems, including decisions about how children would be raised. And when he finally came to realize she didn't care for him the way he cared for her, then what? Sylvia couldn't look into that future without feeling ill.

There was one decision made.

Could she be Fraa Zook?

Willard already knew she had feelings for someone else. Could he stand patiently by, waiting for her to fall out of love with Tobias and into love with him? Could she make a life with a man who would wait ... and wait ... never knowing if she would come to love him as he loved her? Would her future be the same as she would have had with Mark, with a husband who was just as unhappy?

Well, it would be a different future. There would be children, with a house and a thriving business for them to inherit, and an uncle who would love them and teach them all he knew. Sylvia was under no illusions about Hezekiah. She would no more expect him to find somewhere else to live than fly to the moon. The Zook brothers had grown up in that house, as had their father. It was their home.

All right then. She knew that Willard respected her. Trusted her, if introducing her to the bees was any indication.

And no one in the valley held his faith and love for *Gott* more dear. That made a pretty good foundation to build a life on. Of course he was twenty years older than she, and goodness sakes, wouldn't it cause such a flap on the Amish grapevine! It might never recover. But wasn't it better to be talked about because you were getting married than because no one thought you could?

Tobias ... oh, Tobias.

Her whole soul cried out to him. Her throat closed and the tears welled in her eyes once more.

She unclenched her hand from around the poor abused handkerchief, which she'd embroidered with tiny pink-and-white striped carnations, and shook it out to find a dry spot. No one in the household had read about the language of flowers, but she'd once borrowed a library book about it. Into the delicate, tiny petals she'd stitched a silent message, so she could see it every time she used these handkerchiefs. Tobias still had the one she'd lent him earlier, never suspecting what the flowers meant.

I wish I could be with you.

But striped carnations had another meaning. The one she was going to have to remember from this day forward.

I renounce you forever.

Tuesday, June 28

If ever there was a perfect June day, today had been it. Not too hot, and even after supper the air was so gentle that when Tobias rose from the table, he said, "I hate to waste a nice evening. If no one needs the spring wagon, I'd like to get a couple of hours' work done on the Inn's barn."

Sylvia drew in a breath. Here was her chance.

She had made up her mind on Sunday, and said farewell to any future in which Tobias was more than someone to shake hands with after church. She'd prayed without ceasing during the two days since, and no nudge had come from *Gott* to direct her away from this path.

So when the twins clamored to go with him, and he'd agreed that they could, she stopped him at the kitchen door. "Would it be all right if I rode over with you? I'd like to try a new recipe, and it calls for more honey than we have on hand."

He looked a little surprised. "I can pick some up for you."

She shook her head and smiled with what she hoped was friendliness in her eyes, and not a howling wilderness of pain. "Willard will make you choose from among his flavors, and what if you get the wrong one?"

He smiled back. "I'd never want to mess with perfection. You'd be very welcome to come along."

He'd been so nice since Sunday night. Was he trying to make up for blaming her for the muskeg? He must be. He'd apologized to Dat for his rash words, and then had come and apologized to her. It was clear that while he was sorry for the words, he hadn't yet managed to change the opinion that lay behind them. Still, he trusted her enough with the children and that would have to do.

Half a loaf is better than no bread, Mammi Keim used to say. Well, she was about to prove that in more ways than one.

They piled into the wagon, Sylvia once again riding in the back with the saws, tool belt, and the battery-operated screw guns. Tobias let her out at the Zook gate, where she was careful to slip into the front yard without letting any of the roaming chickens escape.

Rhoda clip-clopped on down the road and Sylvia waved good-bye to the twins. Then she took a moment to brace herself for the walk down to the farmhouse. "*Guder owed*, bees," she said to the ones tumbling about in the roses along the fence. "I hope you are well. I've come for some more of your delicious honey."

A trio of bees lifted into the low rays of the sun that burnished their little bodies to gold. They turned a kind of circle in the air before zooming off toward the hives. Maybe it was silly, but she felt ridiculously pleased at the thought that they might have acknowledged her greeting.

The chickens followed her along the neat flagstone path among the flowering elderberry and chokecherry trees. No one tended to come this way to use the front door, but instead went around to the barnyard and the home paddock, where there was a hitching rail, and the back door and the dairy faced each other. But on a soft June evening ... well, if it hadn't been for the actual purpose of her errand, the Zook garden would have positively lent itself to romance.

Willard stepped out onto the porch, a dishtowel in one hand, his eyebrows raised as he watched her stroll closer.

"Don't you all make a picture," he said when she was within earshot. "You and the flowers and the chickens."

Heat prickled into her cheeks. "I hope I didn't interrupt your supper."

He lifted the towel as though indicating supper was over. "*Neh*. Come along in."

"Actually..." Oh goodness. How to put this? "Could we perhaps visit the hives? I wanted to talk something over. And then I'd like another jar of that alfalfa honey, if you still have some."

Something kindled in his eyes and died down before he nodded. "Sure." He leaned inside for a moment, exchanged the towel for a battered straw hat, and joined her.

They walked around the house, then into the goats' meadow and the Miller parcel. From somewhere in the distance, she could hear the shrieks of children. With a chuckle, she said, "Sounds like the twins are testing the temperature of the creek."

"Seems Benny ought to know that already."

"I'm pretty sure he's convinced that glacier melt will warm up eventually. Hope springs eternal."

"That it does."

A moment too late, she realized he didn't mean Benny.

The bees zoomed past them in gold streaks, bringing the last of the day's bounty home to the hive. "I greeted them just now." She needed just one more moment before she said what she had come to say. "I'm positive three of them greeted me back."

"Likely they did. Bees are companionable that way."

They stood in silence for a moment, watching the bees land and hurry into the hive, each one making way for her sisters coming in behind her.

Willard had always seemed to her like a graying, silent chunk of granite, able to stand without speaking for any amount of time as he listened to Aendi Annie meander through one of her stories, or a child stammer out something exciting he had seen in the goat barn. But now, he turned to her after only a minute.

"You had something you wanted to say to me? Zeke is in the house, but I told him to stay there."

He surprised a laugh out of her. "Poor Zeke."

"He didn't mind. He's told me to stay put plenty of times when we're out hunting."

She couldn't put it off any longer. Not with him gazing at her with that expression in his eyes. Hope battling with resignation. "Well ... I've been thinking over what you said last week, when we were standing here."

We. That word again. If only there were another plural that didn't couple two people together so tightly.

"*Ja?* I thought there was a reason to put it by for good."

A good reason. Tobias. "I thought so, too. But it turns out there isn't."

Silence fell as he seemed to think this over. At last, he said, "Feelings usually take a little longer to make a change than a week."

"I—well, I wouldn't know. I just know that mine aren't returned, and so I have to make that change. Take a different path."

"Are you sure they aren't returned?"

She huffed a laugh with no humor in it. "If you heard someone say, *I'm not going to court Willard, and after today, I'm pretty sure I never will,* would you be convinced they meant it?"

"I was pretty sure you meant it last week. And now look."

She let that pass. "The thing is, I'm willing to take that first step. If—if you would still like to court. You may find that we don't get along at all. I may have a hundred annoying habits you can't bear to live with."

"I'll warn you now that I probably have at least that many. And if I don't, Zeke does. Because *mei Bruder* does figure into this, too."

"I know. Every woman in the valley knows."

Somewhere under that beard, he may have chuckled. "And here I thought it was me scaring them off."

"You're not as scary as I used to think when I was a child." She dared to smile at him, but instead of smiling back, his gaze fell to the ground.

"I know I'm too old for you."

"I've been called an old lady by my brothers more than once."

"Even when you're eighty, you won't be an old lady. You have the gift of wonder, and a woman with that will never be old. In body, maybe, but not in spirit."

For one fleeting second, Sylvia felt sorry for the woman who had made the mistake of turning him down some long-ago day in the past. In the next second, speaking of mistakes, she suddenly realized there was one way to erase the memory of Tobias's kiss and put that mistake behind her forever.

"Willard, will you do something for me?"

"Ready to go in for that jar of honey now?"

"In a minute." She took a breath and prepared to shock him. "Will you kiss me?"

He stared at her, frozen to the spot. "What—now?"

"*Ja.* Now."

His eyes never leaving hers, he took a step forward. Then another. His arms came up halfway, then lowered, then he made up his mind and slid them around her. As lightly as a bee landing, his lips touched hers. But when she pressed up to make it a proper kiss, to see if this happened with every man or it was only Tobias she was cursed to remember, he lifted away from her and stepped back.

"Was that what you wanted, Sylvia?"

Not exactly. "It's a beginning. Now, how is Hezekiah going to get back on Sunday if you take me home in your buggy?"

"Are you thinking that I'm going to singing?"

She gave a pretty good impression of a laugh. "*Neh,* I'm thinking that Mamm and Dat and the hands have been invited to Omar Bontragers' for supper. And maybe you and Zeke should get yourselves invited, too."

If the Amish grapevine in the valley had a sturdy stem, it

was made of Omar's niece Susan Bontrager and her mother, his sister-in-law—and the fact that their Bitterroot Dutch Café had become a kind of hub for Amish news. The sensation of Sylvia's going home with Willard Zook would be all over the Siksika by bedtime.

And no one would ever know that Tobias Miller had hurt her badly enough to drive her to such a desperate pass.

❦ 18 ❦

BENNY GASPED and Gracie clapped a hand over his mouth before he yelled and gave them away. She pulled him behind the thick, protective trunk of a Douglas fir. Since the creek was still freezing cold, and no chance of a swim, they'd run up here to visit the goats. Only to get the shock of their lives when Willard had stepped up and kissed Sylvia out of the clear blue.

On the lips! Gracie had expected Sylvia to push him away and read him a lecture to end all lectures for being so fresh. But she had seemed to like it!

Benny craned around one side of the fir, Gracie the other.

Sylvia and Willard rambled back through the goats' meadow, the silly creatures bounding and jumping behind them. Gracie didn't say a word until Willard let Sylvia into the house and it was safe to talk.

"What are we going to do?" she gasped, throwing herself to the grass and ripping up a handful of it to relieve her feelings.

"After all our hard work. What is the matter with her?"

Benny stretched out flat on his back, probably in case he needed to address *der Herr* in this crisis.

"Kissing Willard Zook. Ewwww. He's as old as a *Daadi*!"

"Maybe not to an old maid."

Gracie flung all the pieces of grass at his head. "Don't call her that."

He spat out grass and sat up to brush the rest out of his hair. "We need a plan, for sure and certain. We should go and get Dat."

"And say what? He's still mad at her about the muskeg."

"He can't be mad. He said he was sorry."

"You can say you're sorry and still be mad," Gracie pointed out. "What if we ask her not to let Willard kiss her any more? Oh, my goodness." She flopped back into the grass as her spine gave out with the magnitude of a terrible idea. "He would only kiss her if they were actually courting. And *that* means they might get married. Benny, we have to do something, fast!"

But what exactly they could do was a stumper. Gracie stared through the lacy branches of the firs to the glowing sky directly above. The sun had turned it gold, which meant Dat had about another hour to work. And they had another hour to come up with a plan.

Father, please help us. We want Sylvia for our mother, and I thought that You did, too. What should we do now?

Benny was watching her. "Any answer?" he whispered after a couple of minutes.

She shook her head. "Shh. I'm listening."

A stick snapped on the trail to their left.

Gracie gasped. "Cows!" They weren't allowed near cows, who were notoriously unpredictable and as likely to kick you as come over to greet you.

They both popped up, ready to run, when they saw it wasn't a cow. It was their grandmother.

No, it was an answer from *Gott* Himself.

"Mammi!" Benny jumped a log and ran toward her, Gracie right behind him. "Mammi, we need help."

Mammi's face changed and she pulled Benny to her, hands on his shoulders as she examined him from bare head to bare toes. "Are you all right? Did you fall in? Did a bee sting you?"

"A bee would never sting me. Willard introduced us."

He wrigged out of her grasp and Gracie grabbed her hand. "We saw Willard kissing Sylvia!"

All the concern fell out of Mammi's face and her mouth dropped open in astonishment. She turned and looked across the goats' meadow toward the beehives, and then toward the farmhouse. "Are you for certain sure?"

"*Ja!*" they shouted together. "Right on the lips." Benny made a face.

"Oh my." Lucky thing there was a fallen log handy, for she sat down suddenly. "Oh my. This is unexpected."

"But what are we going to *do*?" Gracie wailed. "What if they get married? How is she going to be our *mamm* then?"

"That is the question of the hour." Mammi seemed to be thinking fiercely. Then she came back to herself. "Does your father know Willard is interested in her?"

"*I* don't know." Gracie climbed onto the log, Benny on the other side of her, and her comforting arms slipped around their backs. "Dat's mad at her about the muskeg."

"The muskeg was hardly her fault. I think he's mad at himself for not knowing what to do—for letting it happen at all. And when people are mad at themselves, it's easy to mistake it for being mad at someone else."

"But how are we going to stop him being mad, and start—" Benny searched for the right word.

"—being in love with her?" Mammi suggested. The two of them nodded. "I think we've come to the point where someone has to tell him what's what."

"Will you help us?" Benny begged. "It's hard to tell grownups what's what. They don't listen."

"And Dat is for sure and certain not going to listen to us," Gracie said unhappily. "We did our best to help him see we wanted Sylvia for our *mamm*, and now look."

"So just to be sure..." Mammi looked from Gracie to her brother, the usual laughter fading from her eyes. "Does this mean you're all right with Sylvia stepping into your mother's place?"

Benny's brow crinkled, clearly wondering what Mamm had to do with this urgent problem. "I ... don't really remember Mamm very much."

"I remember she loved us," Gracie said, trying to be loyal. "Mostly I remember the stories you and Dat tell about her."

Mammi nodded thoughtfully. "All right. Let's go home, and I'll think about how I'm going to help you."

"Don't think too long," Benny warned. "Willard might be in a hurry to get married after waiting all this time."

"And don't forget to tell Dat he kissed Sylvia," Gracie reminded her. "That's important."

"Don't you worry about that." Mammi rose from the log and, each of them holding one of her hands, they walked across the fir needles to the path back to the Inn. "In fact, it might be just the thing to start off with."

❦

With the help of Rob, who was delighted to give Tobias a hand on the last day of his vacation, they got the drywall up and mudded, all ready for painting. After that, all the bunkhouse rooms would need was linoleum flooring.

He washed the drywall dust off his hands and face and walked up the slope to the Inn, feeling as though a couple of hours had been a *gut* day's work. When he walked into the kitchen, he found Susanna alone, pulling a big casserole out of the oven. A salad sat on the table, with slices of fresh home-made bread. Dishes of beet, carrot, and bean pickles made bright spots of red, orange, and green.

"Are you all alone?" he asked. "Where's Mamm?"

"The twins disappeared earlier. I thought they were with you. But she went to look for them."

"I thought they were with *you*. Oh, boy." Apprehension stabbed his stomach. He scrubbed his face with one hand. "Maybe you'd better put that casserole back in. We seem to be missing half the family."

"They can't be far."

"Benny wasn't far when he nearly drowned under that sweeper."

Without a word, she put on the oven mitts and slid the casserole into the oven. "You go look for Mamm, who went to look for *them*, who probably went to look for *Sylvia*."

"Sylvia! They know she's at Zooks'." He glanced at the clock, which inexplicably said quarter to seven. Almost the twins' bedtime, and they hadn't even had supper yet. "Surely she hasn't been there all this time."

"Best get going, and find out."

He didn't waste another second. If the twins were indeed with Sylvia, he was going to have a little talk with her. This couldn't go on. If she was their nanny, then she should put them first. They should have been home two hours ago for their supper, even if he was still down in the barn. If they were all together at Zooks' having a grand old time while poor Susanna was laboring over a hot stove, he was going to—

"Dat!" Benny came running down the creekside path, Gracie right behind him.

"Where have you been?" he demanded, catching up his son and swinging him around before setting him down.

"With Mammi," Gracie said.

And there was his mother, coming along the path in the gloaming looking as serene as if she were in her own garden and his children were already in bed where they were supposed to be.

"Mamm, do you have any idea what time it is?"

She glanced at the watch Dat had given her long before he was born. "Seven minutes to seven. Why? Is the casserole done?"

"Done and back in the oven because no one knew where you all were."

"I knew. Goodness, Tobias, you look like a fire alarm just went off behind you. We're all here and no harm done."

Of course they were. He could see that with his own eyes. "Why didn't the twins have their supper earlier?"

"Because we thought it would be nice if we ate together as a family. Which meant waiting for you to finish work in the barn."

Oh, so his starving children were his own fault?

"We had a snack, Dat." Gracie took his hand and led him along the path. "But I'm hungry now. Did you get the bunkhouse done?"

Why was everyone behaving so normally? "Where is Sylvia?"

The twins looked at each other. Good grief. Had they been to Zooks' or not?

"I expect she's having dinner with Willard," Mamm said calmly.

"She went into the house with him," Benny said. "I thought it was just to get the honey, but Willard and Zeke sure are *gut* cooks. I'd stay if I was invited."

"Me too," Gracie said.

Tobias had had enough. With the Inn in sight through the trees, he let go of the children's hands and jammed his own on his hips. "Why on earth would Sylvia have dinner with Will and Zeke when you *Kinner* haven't had any dinner at all?"

"Your children were with you," Mamm said mildly. "And why wouldn't she have dinner with the man who's courting her? If the children were with us, there's no reason why a grown woman wouldn't accept a man's invitation. Now, come along. It's going to be dark soon."

But Tobias's feet had grown roots and he couldn't have moved if he wanted to. "Wait. What did you say?"

"Which part?"

"About a man courting Sylvia. Who's courting her? What's going on?"

"Willard is," Benny said cheerfully.

"We saw him kiss her," Gracie confided.

"Ewwwww," they both said together, and then laughed like a pair of hyenas.

If someone had swung a cast-iron pan at his head, Tobias wouldn't have been able to duck. He just stood there in the grass, gaping at the three of them. They spoke words that didn't make sense. His brain had frozen just like his mouth.

"Now, children. Kissing is perfectly normal when you're

courting," his mother said. "They thought they were alone, and it was very wrong of you to spy on them."

"We weren't spying!" Benny cried, stung at this injustice. "We were going to see the goats, and there they were in front of the beehives, kissing."

"And then we hid behind a tree. 'Cause kissing is private," Gracie said.

"Would you stop!" Tobias exclaimed. "I don't want to hear another word."

"You did ask," Mamm said, eyeing him as though he were a cow standing in the path. "Well, come along. Susanna will be wondering where we are."

"What about Sylvia?" He flung out an arm in the direction of the Zook place.

His mother shrugged. "What about her? You can pick her up on the way home, can't you?"

"But—but—you said we were eating together as a family."

Mamm gazed at him, faintly puzzled. "*We* are. But you've never really included Sylvia as part of the family. She's an employee. The children's nanny. The poor girl is entitled to a life of her own—and besides, they've likely already finished dinner. I wonder what they're having for dessert." She turned to start for home. "Come on, you two. Last one in is a rotten egg."

They took off, Mamm bringing up the rear at a fast clip, her dark green skirts swishing around her legs. Tobias stood in the gloom under the trees, her words ringing in his ears.

You've never really included Sylvia as part of the family.

And like the pages of one of the twins' picture books, images from the last couple of weeks turned over before his mind's eye.

Sylvia, nursing Benny as tenderly as any mother after his ordeal in the creek.

Gracie, begging him to let her look after them.

Sylvia and Gracie covered in cake at the barn raising, laughing at themselves like they would never stop.

Both his children covered in mud. Sylvia throwing Benny to safety in a superhuman effort that put herself at risk.

And he, Tobias, blaming her. Repeatedly. Even when she didn't deserve it. *"Ach, du Lieva,"* he groaned, sinking to the grass, his head in his hands. Why had he done it? What *Deifel* inside him had gone out of its way to push her as far from him as it could?

Because you're ashamed.

He rested his forehead on his knees.

Yes. He was ashamed. Ashamed that he hadn't noticed Lily Anne's condition before it was too late to do anything about it. Ashamed that he'd betrayed her memory by noticing Sylvia walking across the yard after church, noticing the way the sun fell across her cheek and made spiky shadows under her lashes. Noticing how loving she was with his children, even before he'd hired her out of desperation at his inability to be a proper father to them.

Noticing the sweetness of her lips when she'd kissed him.

With a groan, he gently banged his forehead on his knees.

Noticed? That kiss had been a lightning bolt from heaven itself. He'd wanted to pull her in, drink her in, kiss her until neither of them could breathe. And instead he'd pushed her away, distanced himself from her in any way he could.

Because he was afraid.

He didn't trust himself to be a good husband. He had failed so miserably with Lily Anne that he couldn't risk loving another woman and watching history repeat itself. Not with him. Not with someone so unworthy.

"Ach, mei Liebe." Lily Anne's voice whispered on the wind of memory, straight from the hospital room that final night, before she went into surgery and he had never seen her again outside her coffin. "My dearest love, of course you're worthy. Never blame yourself. I want you to be brave for our *Kinner*, and some day, you'll find a woman who is as worthy of you as you are of her." Her voice had faded, along with her strength. "I bless her already for making you and Benny and Gracie happy. I do, truly. I love you with all my heart ... we both do. That woman ... and me."

Those had been her last words. And he had deliberately wiped them from his mind, vowing he would never marry again, never put a woman in such danger.

Sylvia can pull herself out of danger. She's already proved that.

For a person who was so soft and comforting, she had a core of steel that glimmered out when it was needed. Like on the road in that storm, grabbing the reins of a runaway horse. And in the aftermath, as though riding on that surge of bravery, kissing him as though it was the only thing that mattered in the world.

"She doesn't love Willard Zook." He lifted his head when someone spoke, and then realized it had been himself. "You don't kiss like that—care like that—risk your life like that unless ..." The truth hit him with a thump, right in the heart. "She loves *me*." The words caught in his throat. "And I love her. Lily Anne, you were right. I'm the last man who's worthy of her. But I'm not going to let her go."

He scrambled to his feet and set off into the woods at a dead run.

BENNY GRABBED GRACIE'S SHOULDER. "THERE HE GOES."

They were sitting on the veranda, where she was saying *guder nacht* to Sunny the chicken, cuddling her in both arms. Sunny was an armful, and it took both to hold her. Gracie let out a long breath of relief that their father was finally seeing the light, and put the bird down. Sunny, who didn't like the twilight when the coyotes were out, hurried across the patio to the coop where her family was safe inside.

"We better tell Mammi to put a plate in the oven for him," Gracie said, with the satisfied air of a job well done. "Who knows when he'll be back."

❦ 19 ❧

Her stomach might be pleasantly full of a delicious dinner of ribs and salad and cauliflower with goat-cheese sauce, but Sylvia had eaten it to be a good guest, not because she had an appetite. How could she think about food when inside her head was a maelstrom of indecision and pain? This dinner was one of the most uncomfortable she had ever sat through, and that was saying something, considering how long her mother had been trying to get her married off.

Finally, when Zeke had told them he would take care of the dishes and they might button up the goats for the night if they wanted something to do, Sylvia realized what this uneasiness meant.

What was it the Psalmist had said? *Thou wilt shew me the path of life: in thy presence is fulness of joy.* Except in her case, never mind full—the joy was missing altogether. She had taken a wrong path for all the wrong reasons, and was no longer in His presence. She had fallen out of the circle of *Gottes wille*. It had never happened to her before, and she was quickly learning just how terrifying a place it could be.

She could not live in that place. Cost her what it may, she had to free herself.

Lieber Gott, thank You for showing me in time. Give me the words. I don't want to break this good man's heart.

She helped Willard chivvy the goats into the barn and top up their feed. When he closed the barn door behind them, the urgency inside told her she couldn't waste another moment.

"Willard, I must tell you something."

He gazed at her, his eyes catching the last of the day's light through the pines. And in those eyes, she saw the kind of pain that told her somehow, he already knew.

"I—I've lost my peace," she said. How did a person begin when it meant the end?

"I know," he said simply. "I saw it at dinner. A woman sat at our table, but she wasn't the same one who came walking through the garden in the sunshine."

"I'm so sorry," she choked. "I thought I could care for you —I *do* care, only not in the way a woman should. For her ... her future husband." Her voice wobbled, and her throat closed, and somehow she was crying against his chest while he patted her awkwardly on the back.

Finally she found the strength to stand on her own two feet, and pulled yet another embroidered handkerchief out of her apron to blow her nose. She saw him gazing at the delicate border of flowers. "Carnations," she said with a cracked little laugh.

"I renounce you forever," he said, shocking her to the core that he would know such a thing. "I should have known when you used it for a potholder earlier."

"Please forgive me." She crumpled up the tattletale hanky and stuck it in her apron pocket.

"Of course I forgive you. I'm disappointed," he added. "I

knew your heart wasn't free, but I was willing to take the chance when you came back today. Can't blame a man for trying."

"*Neh*, I surely can't." With a wobbly attempt at a smile, she found the courage to meet his eyes once more. "I know it's too much to ask, but ... I meant what I said before. I don't have so many *gut* friends that I can afford to give one away. I still want to ... be that, at least. Despite everything."

"It isn't too much to ask. I would have asked if you hadn't beat me to it. I wish you well, Sylvia. I wish you every happiness you're hoping for."

"It's a vain hope," she admitted bluntly. "He's already made that plain. But I can't offer you half a heart, either. It's got to be whole, whether I have anyone to give it to or not."

"You're wise as well as loving and kind."

A blush prickled into her cheeks. "So are you." She held out a hand. *"Guder nacht, mei Freind."*

"*Guder nacht*, Sylvia. Give them my greetings at the Inn."

She squeezed his hand and left him there, feeling his gaze as he watched her safely onto the path.

She did not hear him whisper, soft as branches rustling on the wind, *"Guder nacht, mei Liebe."* Nor did she see the dampness in his eyes as he turned and walked slowly through the meadow to the house.

THIS FAR NORTH, THE LIGHT OF DAY LINGERED WELL INTO the evening. Sylvia's feet were sure on the path as she hurried along the creek, and her heart was so light she thought she might just burst and fly up into the glowing sky. She was back within God's will once more, though retracing her steps to that place had been the hardest thing she had ever done.

Let him find peace, Lord. If it be Thy will, I pray that You would send Willard happiness. Bring the one You mean for him, and even if I never know earthly love, with all he has to offer a woman, he deserves Your gift.

Into her prayer came a sound—the sound of pounding feet. A man. Running. Coming to the Zook farm for help? With a sharp intake of breath, she flung a prayer for the safety of those at the Inn toward heaven, and peered down the path.

And then he ran into the clearing where she stood and her heart gave its usual thump of recognition. "Tobias! Is everything all right?"

He skidded to a halt, panting. "Sylvia?" It was almost as though he did not recognize her.

"I was just coming." It was an effort to sound normal. "Are you all ready to leave?"

"*Ja. Neh.* I don't know whether I'm coming or going." He bent over, hands braced on his knees as he gasped for breath.

Good heavens. Alarm arrowed through her blood, right to her fingertips. "Has something happened to the twins? Tobias, you're scaring me."

"I guess you could say so." He laughed, a broken sound, and straightened to look her in the eye. "They saw you kissing Willard Zook."

Words backed up in her throat like a logjam and rendered her speechless. How...? Where...?

"Is it true? Are you courting? Are you going to marry him?"

What's it to you?

You don't want me.

It's none of your business.

She could have said those things, and they would have been the truth. But her heart held a different truth that demanded to be spoken. "Not any more. I broke it off just now. And broke the poor man's heart."

His breathing hitched. "Why did you do that?"

Because I love you, even though you don't love me.

"Because I lost my peace." But that wasn't the whole truth. "He knows there's someone else. He knew he would have been taking me with a heart that wasn't whole. And in the end, I couldn't do that to him."

"There's someone else?" A light kindled in his eyes that had nothing to do with the last of the light in the clearing.

"Of course," she said simply. "You." She waved a deprecating hand. "Oh, I know you don't feel the same way. I know you don't plan to marry again. But I couldn't marry Willard, even if it means being alone. He doesn't deserve that."

"How do you know I don't feel the same way?" He took a step closer, bringing them within arms' reach.

"I heard you. The other day in the barn. *I'm not going to court Sylvia,* you said. *And I'm pretty sure I never will.*"

She had silenced him with his own words.

And then she was shocked into silence, too, when he took both her cold hands and held them in his warm ones.

"I am the greatest, blindest fool that *Gott* ever made," he said quietly. "And if you'll forgive me—for those words and a hundred others—I will spend the rest of my life making it up to you. Serving you as a man serves the woman he loves. Putting you first. Seeking your counsel. Loving you."

Still she could not speak. This couldn't be happening. Tobias Miller couldn't be standing here telling her he loved her when she'd heard him say the opposite with her own ears.

"I know I have a long way to go to earn your forgiveness," he said, as though reading the disbelief in her eyes. His hands tightened around hers. "I said terrible things—things that weren't true. I suppose I was saying them to myself. Sylvia, I'm the one who put my twins in danger by letting them go out on the muskeg without checking it first. I'm the one who didn't know what to do—who had to watch you risk your own safety to go out there and save Benny. I've been a terrible friend. You'd be justified in telling me to take my children and get out of your life forever." He ran out of breath and dragged in a lungful of air. "But I hope you won't. I hope you'll let me court you properly. Love you properly. Please."

Of all the thoughts flapping frantically in her head, one finally found a place to land. "But you love Lily Anne. Your heart isn't whole, either."

He shook his head. "*Gott* has taken her to Himself ... and He has brought me to you. He spoke to me in no uncertain terms tonight, and the scales fell from my eyes. All this time, you've been right here, standing in a mother's place, a wife's place, and I didn't see it until now. Please tell me I'm not too late. Please tell me that in saying no to Willard, you haven't said no to me as well."

"*Neh,*" she whispered. "I haven't."

"Can I be a part of your life, Sylvia? Will you let me court you?"

"I think I'm past that."

"If you mean you're too old for courting, then I'd better tell you that I'm staring thirty in the face from a lot closer than you."

She laughed, and her frozen mind and body seemed to shed its coat of ice in a warm current of joy. "I meant I skipped past courting months ago." Boldly, she moved his hands to her waist and dared to link hers around his neck. "I'm already at the loving part."

In the shadows under the trees, his eyes were deep pools of

love with a sparkle of dawning happiness. "And will you let me love you? I can't promise I'll be a perfect husband, but I'll love you with all my heart and strength every day."

"I am far from perfect," she confessed. "But as long as two imperfect people stand within *Gottes wille*, then they are safe and blessed. I love you, Tobias. I want to be your wife, and the twins' mother. And whatever His will is for us in the future, I want that, too."

He buried his face in the hollow where her neck met her shoulder. "I love you, *mei Liebe*. I know that beyond a shadow of turning. I want to spend every day with you for as long as *Gott* allows us."

He found her lips, and in his kiss she felt the truth of his love and the warmth of his promise. And when at last he released her, he took her hand, his fingers twining with hers. They walked slowly down the path toward the Inn, where the last of the sunlight flickered through the trees, lighting the path ahead with joy.

EPILOGUE
WILD ROSE AMISH INN

Friday, July 1

Dear cousin Emily,

Thank you for your last letter and all its news of the family on Prince Edward Island. How exciting that your buddy bunch has got its quilting group back together! While I will never be a quilter like you or our cousin Malena, I do enjoy it. And now that I'm making things for my hope chest, I feel as though I have good reason to go to Rose Garden Quilts and look at all the pretty fabric just a little more often.

We have had some doings around here! We had a barn raising a month ago, which the guests here at the Inn enjoyed watching. A couple of them even pitched in to help. That same week, my nephew Benny fell in the creek and was caught under a sweeper. Luckily Tobias found him in time ... and one of the fishermen happened to be a nurse, so he was well looked after.

Stephen and I have been making plans since we got

engaged. We've spoken to the bishop and will very likely marry around the same time as Mom and Luke, so that the bench wagon doesn't have to move :) It can't be soon enough for me —you know how long I've been waiting! We're not just sure yet where we're going to live, since he's working about five miles away. But there is time enough to figure that out.

Speaking of love in the air, Tobias is courting Sylvia Keim, whose father owns the Bow K Ranch where Stephen is foreman. Tobias has been working there, too, after two of the hands had to go home to Colorado. And you would not believe it, but it turns out that Gracie and Benny have been matchmaking the two of them! You should see those kids—they are so fond of Sylvia and only Tobias and my mother are happier about the courtship than they are. I have to confess that it took me a little while to warm up to Sylvia. Maybe it was because everyone thought we ought to be best friends right off the bat, and I took exception to it. But now that she's going to be my sister-in-law, I can see why the twins love her. She certainly loves them like they were her own. It will be so wonderful to have another woman in the family, with all these menfolk!

My brothers Gideon and Seth are well, working on the Circle M Ranch. They are cowboys through and through. My romantic heart wishes that they could find The One like Tobias and I have. Maybe I'll take a page from the twins' book and try my hand at a little matchmaking. Don't you think it's time that Gideon settled down? He's a bit of an individual, but that would only keep life interesting, wouldn't it? There are lots of nice girls in the valley. The only ones I would leave off the list would be Sylvia's cousins Bethany and Sharon, who will be going home at the end of August, and the Yoder girls. I would not wish Calvin or Dave Yoder as brothers-in-law on anybody—especially not one of my brothers!

Oh, one little piece of news ... remember Patricia King, Noah's sister? She's started work at Rose Garden Quilts. Rose says that she has a gift for helping people find just the right fabrics, which leaves Rose free to manage the shop and the accounts. Patricia and her family are in the other church district, but with her brother married to our cousin Rebecca, I hope to see more of her over on this side soon. Hmm ... maybe she would make a good match for Gideon? Anyway, Noah has the foundation poured for his and Rebecca's house and the carpentry shop, so knowing him, it wouldn't surprise me if they were ready to move in by the time the snow flies.

Snow. What am I thinking? I'd much rather enjoy this beautiful Montana summer. We're having a barbecue tonight to celebrate Tobias and Sylvia, so there will be quite a crowd—the Circle M folks, the Kings, my mother's cousins the Zook brothers, and the Keims. It will be fun, and of course, our half dozen guests from the Inn will be welcome as well. Perhaps my career as a matchmaker may begin as soon as tonight! Ha ha.

I'll let this do for now. Wish you were here to eat ribs and elk chili with us! I know that your heart is mending now after being mistreated so much, but it would sure be nice to give you a hug all the same. Greetings and love to your family from Mom and Luke and all of us.

With love, your cousin and sister in Christ,
Susanna

THE END

AFTERWORD
A NOTE FROM ADINA

I hope you've enjoyed the ninth book about the Miller family on the Circle M Ranch and at the Wild Rose Amish Inn. If you subscribe to my newsletter, you'll hear about new releases in the series, my research in Montana, and snippets about quilting and writing and chickens—my favorite subjects!

I hope you'll join me by subscribing at https://www.subscribepage.com/shelley-adina.

Haven't read the first book in the Amish Cowboys of Montana? Pick up *The Amish Cowboy* on my store at https://www.moonshellbooks.com. And while you're there, be sure to browse my other Amish novels set in beautiful Whinburg Township, Pennsylvania, beginning with *The Wounded Heart*.

Following is a glossary of the Pennsylvania Dutch words used in this book. But first, here's a sneak peek at *The Amish Cowboy's Wedding Quilt*, Gideon and Patricia's story!

The Amish Cowboy's Wedding Quilt
© Adina Senft

If the grass looks greener on the other side of the fence, water and fertilize your own side. —Mountain Home Amish proverb

Patricia King has made up her mind to spend the summer on *Rumspringe*—just for a few months, to get a taste of *Englisch* life and have some fun outside her parents' strict rules. She loves her new job at Rose Garden Quilts, partly because it brings her into contact with people from all walks of *Englisch* life—people like the Madison boys at the Rocking Diamond dude ranch, who aren't afraid to show what they feel and say what they think. What's the harm in accepting a date with one of them, if she's discreet? If only she hadn't made the mistake of confiding in Gideon Miller. Now he won't mind his own business, and worse, his sister Susanna thinks she and Gideon would make a perfect match!

Gideon was baptized into the church a few years ago, and has no desire to be anything but an Amish cowboy right here in the Siksika Valley. It drives him crazy that a kind, talented girl like Patricia is so set on testing the boundaries of the Amish faith—to say nothing of getting involved with *Englisch* folks who don't have her best interests at heart. He finds reasons to spend time in town, dropping in to see her—as a friend, of course. He can't seem to stay away, can't stifle these protective feelings ... and can't admit his sister might be right and they mean more than friendship.

The more he tries to be her friend, the more Patricia wants to run. Until one wrong decision upends both their lives ... and Gideon becomes the only person Patricia can turn to for help.

The Montana Millers. They believe in faith, family, and the land. They'll need all three when love comes to Mountain Home!

Find your copy of The Amish Cowboy's Wedding Quilt at your favorite online retailer, or at moonshellbooks.com!

GLOSSARY

Spelling and definitions from Eugene S. Stine, *Pennsylvania German Dictionary* (Birdboro, PA: Pennsylvania German Society, 1996).

Words used:

Aendi: auntie

Bischt du okay? Are you okay?

Boppli(n): baby, babies

Bruder: brother

Daadi: grandfather

Dat: Dad

Deifel: devil

Denki, denkes: thank you, thanks

Dochder(e): daughter, daughters

Druwwel: trouble

Englisch: not-Amish people, English language

Englischer: English person

der Herr: the Lord

Fraa: wife

Gmay: congregation, church body

Gott: God

Gott in Himmel: God in heaven

Gottes wille: God's will

Grischtdaag: Christmas

Grossmammi: great-grandmother

Guder mariye: Good morning

Guder nacht: Good night

Guder owed: Good afternoon/evening

gut: good

Haus: house

ja: yes

Kaffee: coffee

Kapp: women's prayer covering

Kind, Kinner: child, children

kumm mit: come along (lit. come with)

Kumm mit: Come with me.

Liebe: love

Lieber Gott in Himmel: dear God in Heaven

Liebling: little love

Liewi: dear

Maedsche(r): girl, girls

Mamm: Mom

Mammi: Grandma

mei: my

Middaag: midday

Narr: idiot

neh: no

Nix? From *nichts,* Is it not?

Onkel: uncle

Schulhaus: schoolhouse

Sohn: son

verhuddelt: confused, mixed up
Verschteh? Understand?
Verschtanne: We understand
wunderbaar: wonderful
Youngie: young people

The Highest Mountain

The Sweetest Song

The Heart's Return (novella)

❦

Breaking Faith

Grounds to Believe

Pocketful of Pearls

Sounds in the Night

Over Her Head

❦

Glory Prep (faith-based young adult)

Glory Prep

The Fruit of My Lipstick

Be Strong and Curvaceous

Who Made You a Princess?

Tidings of Great Boys

The Chic Shall Inherit the Earth

ABOUT THE AUTHOR

USA Today bestselling author Adina Senft grew up in a plain house church, where she was often asked by outsiders if she was Amish (the answer was no). She holds a PhD in Creative Writing from Lancaster University in the UK. Adina was the winner of RWA's RITA Award for Best Inspirational Novel in 2005 for *Grounds to Believe*, a finalist for that award in 2006 for *Pocketful of Pearls*, and was a Christy Award finalist in 2009 for *The Fruit of My Lipstick*. She appeared in the 2016 documentary film *Love Between the Covers*, is a popular speaker and convention panelist, and has been a guest on many podcasts, including Worldshapers and Realm of Books.

She writes steampunk adventure and mystery as Shelley Adina; and as Charlotte Henry, writes classic Regency romance. When she's not writing, Adina is usually quilting, sewing historical costumes, or enjoying the garden with her flock of rescued chickens.

Adina loves to talk with readers about books, quilting, and chickens!
www.moonshellbooks.com